**ANSKY, S. The dybbuk; between two worlds, tr. and with an intro. by
S. Morris Engel. Nash, 1975 (c1974). 157p il 74-82063. 7.95.
ISBN 0-8402-1356-5**

At $7.95 for a volume containing one play, this is a genuine luxury edi-
tion, but it is a beautiful one. Ansky's classical Yiddish play, written
early in the 20th century, is beautifully translated and elegantly il-
lumined. The illustrations by Jennifer Coleman, biographical and in-
troductory notes by the translator S. Morris Engel, and even the original musical accompaniment make this a very attractive volume.
Ansky's play is one of the modern classics of standard repertory
theater. This new translation gives the play a freshness which will
make it even more appealing. Although this is not for the library on a
tight budget, if your library is going to have one edition of *The
dybbuk,* let it be this one. For all drama libraries, undergraduate and
graduate collections.

* *Rappoport, Solomon*

the Dybbuk

S. Morris Engel was born in Poland but studied as a rabbinical student in Toronto, Montreal, and New York. He later received degrees from various Canadian universities in literature and philosophy. He is currently a professor of philosophy at the University of Southern California. Dr. Engel has translated Rakmil Bryks' *A Cat in the Ghetto,* and is the author of a number of books including *The Problem of Tragedy* and *Wittgenstein's Doctrine of the Tyranny of Language.* He resides in Los Angeles with his wife and two sons.

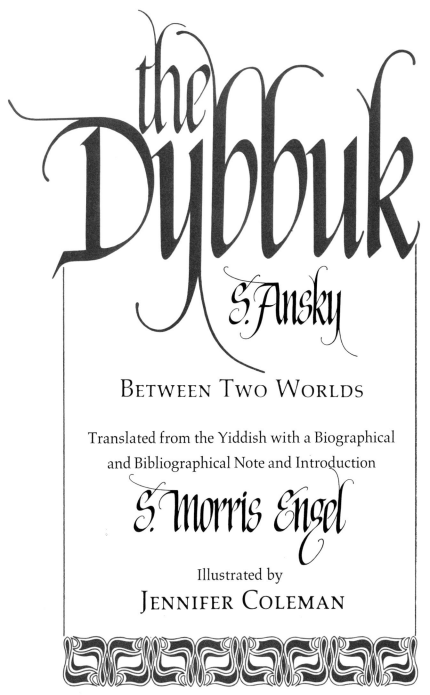

the Dybbuk

S. Ansky

BETWEEN TWO WORLDS

Translated from the Yiddish with a Biographical
and Bibliographical Note and Introduction

S. Morris Engel

Illustrated by
JENNIFER COLEMAN

NASH PUBLISHING, LOS ANGELES

Other Books by S. Morris Engel

The Problem of Tragedy
Language and Illumination
Wittgenstein's Doctrine of the Tyranny of Language
and essays and reviews in various scholarly journals

Translation: A Cat in the Ghetto by Rachmiel Bryks

Copyright 1974 © by S. Morris Engel

Library of Congress Catalog Card Number: 74-82063
International Standard Book Number: 0-8402-1356-5

Published simultaneously in the United States and Canada
by Nash Publishing Corporation, 9255 Sunset Boulevard
Los Angeles, California 90069

Printed in the United States of America

First Printing

To Faegel—Again

Preface

Shloyme Zanvl Rappoport, known throughout the literary world under the pseudonym of S. Ansky, was born in Vitebsk, Russia, in 1863. He led a life of wandering, roaming the cities and villages of Russia, collecting folktales and writing the tragic history of his people. *The Dybbuk,* which is a product of these travels, is the only complete dramatic piece he ever wrote. The play was written before the outbreak of the First World War; its first performance had to wait, however, until 1920. Ansky, unfortunately, did not live to see it mounted onstage. He died, on November 8, 1920, shortly before its first performance. His collected works—including among them his unfinished play *Day and Night*—appeared in Yiddish in 15 volumes (Warsaw, 1920-25).

7

Ansky wrote the first version of *The Dybbuk* in Russian. He gave the manuscript to Stanislavsky, the great Russian director of the Moscow Art Theatre, who praised it highly and advised him to rewrite the play in Yiddish and have it performed by a Jewish troupe. It was also on the advice of Stanislavsky that the character of the Messenger was introduced. The Yiddish version soon appeared, and it in turn was rendered into classical Hebrew by the great Hebrew poet, Chaim Nachman Bialik. Ansky so admired this translation of his work that when he subsequently lost his own Yiddish original he translated the play back to Yiddish from Bialik's Hebrew version.

The play became extremely popular after Ansky's death and was performed by both professional and amateur troupes throughout the civilized world. A year after its premiere at the Elyseum Theatre in Warsaw on December 9, 1920—which marked the end of the traditional thirty-day period of mourning that followed Ansky's death on November 9—it was produced by Maurice Schwartz in New York's Yiddish Art Theatre, and several months later, it was staged in Moscow, in Hebrew, by the Habima Troupe under the direction of Stanislavsky's gifted pupil Eugene Vakhtangov. (By May 1928 the

Habima celebrated the 600th performance of the play). Three years later, on December 15, 1925, an English version by Henry G. Alsberg and Winifred Katzin, directed by David Vardi of the Habima, was given at the Neighborhood Playhouse. With Mary Ellis as Laia, supported by Albert Carroll and Dorothy Sands, this production moved uptown to Broadway in 1926 and then continued on to a national tour. Among the more recent New York revivals of *The Dybbuk* are the Equity Library production in English in 1947, and a Hebrew version again, by the visiting Habima players, in 1948. In 1954 it was revived once again by David Ross at the Fourth Street Theater. The leading members of that cast—Theodore Bikel, Ludwig Donath, Jack Guilford—with the addition of Carol Lawrence in the role of Laia, were again seen in the television version in 1960-61 which Sidney Lumet directed for the Play of the Week series. This was not the play's first filmed presentation: in 1934 the drama was made into a Yiddish film, produced in Poland; and more recently, in 1970, an Israeli film of *The Dybbuk* featured David Opatoshu, Peter Frye, and Tina Wodetzky.

The play's musical history is no less remarkable. Joel Engel's music dates from 1912 when Ansky and

Engel, who were close friends and collaborators, first heard the old folk tale from an innkeeper's wife. Basing his play on this folk tale, Ansky constructed the drama on the leitmotif of the Hassidic melody *mipnei mah* ("Wherefore, O wherefore?") The melody (reprinted here as published in the Yiddish edition of the play) was used at the first performance of the play and formed part of the stage music composed by Engel which he later published as his *Suite "Hadibuk"* (Op. 35).

In 1929, three years after the appearance of Engel's *Suite,* Bernard Sekles wrote an orchestral prelude entitled *Der Dybuk. Il Dibuk* was composed in 1934 by the Italian composer Lodovico Rocco and made its bow at La Scala in Milan on March 24, 1934, and in New York in 1936. Another opera based on the play, composed by David Tamkin, had its world premiere at the New York City Center on October 4, 1951; and still a third opera by another American composer, Michael White, had its premiere in Seattle in the spring of 1963. In addition, the play has formed the basis of at least two ballets: one by Max Ettinger in 1947 and another, more recently by Jerome Robbins, with music by Leonard Bernstein, which premiered only this spring (1974) at the Lincoln Center in New York.

Although extremely popular among theatergoers and newspaper reviewers, *The Dybbuk* was somehow neglected by literary critics. Furthur information, however, regarding both the author and the drama may be found in the *Universal Jewish Encyclopedia*, Volume 9; the *Encyclopedia Judaica*, Volumes 3 and 6; and in Joseph T. Shipley's *Guide to Great Plays* (1956). A more detailed discussion of the play as an art form is contained in *The Drama of Transition* by I. Goldberg (Cincinnati: Steward Kidd, Co., 1922); and in A.A. Roback's *The Story of Yiddish Literature* (New York: Yiddish Scientific Institute, 1940). *The Nation* for January 6, 1926, and *New Republic* for January 5, 1927 carry extensive reviews of the first productions of the play.

It is perhaps interesting that the psychoanalytic approach, which still seems to permeate the very air we breathe, did not fail to enter the world of this drama and offer its interpretation. Ansky, it is argued, suffered from an Oedipus complex, and *The Dybbuk* is the psychological resolution or record of this conflict which raged in his soul. The argument is that Ansky seems to have identified himself with Khonnon, and Khonnon's love for Laia was in reality Ansky's love for his own mother, whom

Laia represents in the drama. In addition, Laia's mother in the drama is called Khanne, the very name of Ansky's own mother, Anna—a name which (revealingly, it is argued by these interpreters) Ansky incorporated into his own name when he adopted a pseudonym.

A word, finally, about this translation and edition of *The Dybbuk.*

What the reader has here is a revised version of a work first undertaken and published over twenty years ago. It would be good to be able to say that in being interested in this play then—dealing as it does with the supernatural and having as its central drama an exorcism—I was some two decades ahead of my time. But this would not be true.

I came to the play by a rather different route. I had been pursuing talmudic studies for some years when it gradually became clearer and clearer to me that my interests lay elsewhere. Abandoning these studies, I entered the university and submerged myself in the study of literature. Because my background and education had been entirely religiously oriented, I was even then still ignorant that there existed (or even that there *could* exist) a serious, secular Jewish literature. Then one day, as these

things often happen, I chanced to walk into the small Jewish library in my hometown in Winnipeg, Canada, and, browsing through the display, I came upon an old, worn copy of *The Dybbuk*. For reasons I did not then fully understand, I found myself powerfully moved and stirred by what I read. While deeply stirred thus, I resolved to make this, and other works like it, available to those who, like me, were ignorant of their very existence.

Although, as with so many other things in my life, I was far from realizing all the hopes I had then fondly envisioned for it and myself, I have never regretted that decision—all the less so now that it is once again being allowed to see the light of day. For this I am deeply grateful to Mr. Eric Lasher, president of Nash, whose own decision to publish a new translation of *The Dybbuk* was arrived at almost at the same moment my letter of enquiry soliciting his interest reached his desk; and to his editor, Mrs. Ruth Glushanok, whose knowledge of literature, joy in life, and love of things Jewish once again transformed this undertaking for me into a labor of love.

S. Morris Engel
Los Angeles, California
March 31, 1974

Introduction

It can hardly be said that *The Dybbuk* is the product of one mind or even of one hand. Into its composition went the best and also the worst elements of the experiences of an entire people: their suffering, their superstitions, their culture, and their soul. In this drama, Ansky has not so much produced a work of art on the lines of certain forms and conventions, as he has wandered through the lonely and dim streets of the towns of eastern Europe, chosen a beggar here, a scholar there, a hunchback, and commanded them to ascend the elevation of the theater for the better view of the spectator. In this play, then, life of a community, of a social group, nay, life itself, is made to reveal its disturbing and soul-stirring drama. *The Dybbuk* is in essence a myth.

It is for this reason that *The Dybbuk* has always been a most popular play among all peoples. Its closeness to the experiences of the individual and collective soul has made it a rallying point around which people of all faiths and backgrounds have gathered to be overwhelmed by its power and intensity. It is perhaps for this same reason that little criticism has been directed toward its interpretation. This is most unfortunate. The play's extreme lack of sophistication, its naivete, its seeming vulgarity have, for too long a time, closed it off from the literary world.

There is, perhaps, another reason why this tragedy has been so little discussed by critics, a reason that stems from the very nature of the play itself. *The Dybbuk* has as its source and fountainspring a body of facts and experiences that are not a part of the mainstream of Western civilization, making it difficult for an outsider, or one who has traveled only on the mainstream, to appreciate fully the vast implications and beauty of the play. This, however, should not deter us from very closely examining its background in order to appreciate the end result. It is not unusual for artists to create a system of their own and then produce an artistic work on the basis of that system, as was the case,

for example, with Joyce and Yeats. Ansky, however, did not create a system of his own, but adapted one that already existed among his people. A closer examination of the basic facts of the drama would reveal, nonetheless, that the experiences presented, the characters delineated, are really not isolated and individual, but, rather, symbolic of the elemental and primitive. People of all faiths and persuasions have always found themselves powerfully attracted to these aspects of the play.

*   *   *

The outer action of the drama, from its first to its last movement, takes place in or around some religious establishment and thus strikes the keynote of the entire play: the influence of a heavenly or hellish host on an earthbound folk. This, of course, is what was intimated in the title originally given to the play by its author, *Between Two Worlds.* The play is not entirely concerned with a religious or mystic theme, however, although this forms a great part of the experiences dramatized. The air of mysticism that pervades the entire production acts only as the enveloping or guiding force under which the characters of the play lead their existence. The characters themselves are entirely human and consequently highly tragic.

17

The setting is a *shtetl* in eastern Europe, a ghetto to which its inhabitants were—with rare exceptions—restricted to live out their lives. It was a world not often disturbed by the outside, unless by a pogrom or, occasionally, by a member of the community who left the ghetto by the route of conversion. Most of the Jews who lived here were poor and on the whole not educated, although every Jewish child was required by the Law to know at least the rudiments of reading and writing in Hebrew or Yiddish in order to follow the prayers.

It is no wonder that Hassidism, an eighteenth-century sect founded in eastern Europe, should have had such a great appeal for them. The Baal Shem Tov, the founder of this movement, taught that all are equal before God, and that God encompassed all things. No man or thing, therefore, must be despised; whether good or wicked, man's function was to redeem the evil in nature by bringing it within God's Light. Hassidism taught that man could achieve communion with God not solely by way of study—as had been believed by tradition—but also through prayer, dance, and song. Placing stress upon the heart rather than the intellect, Hassidim preached that the ideal worship of God was through simplicity and sincerity: God could be

worshipped while in the woods, or on the road, no
less acceptably than in the synagogue. Nor need
one's prayers be clothed in words in order to reach
God. What was essential was that man's heart be
attuned to God and be filled with love and joy.

Discarding the learned discourse, the Hassidic *rebbe*
or sage taught his disciples by way of stories and
parables. Drawing heavily upon the Kabbala—a
body of mystical thought whose origins go back as
far as the first century B.C.—he imbued his
disciples with a renewed sense of the wonder and
mystery of the world which God created. Communion with God, he taught, is open to all, ultimate
union coming with the perfection of one's soul.

But to return to our play:

Before the curtain rises on the first act, a soft, mystic
chant is heard coming from a corner of the dark
stage:

> *Wherefore, O wherefore*
> *Has the soul*
> *Fallen from exalted heights*
> *To profoundest depths?*
> *Within itself, the fall*
> *Contains the ascension.*

The curtain is raised and the sand in the hourglass begins to fall. When the curtain is lowered at the end of the drama the same soft, mystic chant is heard again, but, in the meantime, the action of the play has already covered both the fall and the redemption.

Khonnon, a poverty-stricken but brilliant talmudic scholar, falls in love with Laia, the daughter of a rich merchant at whose house he had been a guest for a period of time. The feeling of love between the two young people is mutual, but its consummation in marriage is prevented by the girl's father, named Sender, who, following European custom, seeks a rich suitor for his daughter.

Half-crazed by his passion for Laia, and driven to desperation by the vague feeling that Laia is his predestined bride, Khonnon takes to the study of the Kabbala, a system of Hebrew mysticism wherein the eternal secrets and powers of the universe are reputed to be revealed. In the Kabbala Khonnon hopes to find confirmation for his presentiment, and to gain the power to bring it to fulfillment. He becomes so immersed in the study of this mystic work that every external action appears to him a sign of his growing power over destiny. But the deeper he progresses in his study of the Kabbala and

numerology, and the more convinced he becomes of his growing power over external events, the more he loses contact with the real world. He finds himself rejecting the Talmud, or at least that part of it which is concerned with Law, which he finds cold and meaningless. The Song of Songs he comes to regard not as a symbolic work but a personal one, and is unable to recite it without reading his own fate into it: instead of being true to the original by singing, "Behold, thou art fair, my beloved," he sings, "Behold, thou art fair, my *predestined.*" Finally, Sender's repeated failure to come to terms with the numerous suitors for Laia's hand reassures him that his preoccupation with the Kabbala has not been fruitless. Consequently, when Sender announces that he has at last come to terms with one of these suitors, the kabbalistic world in which Khonnon has been living crushes him, and he falls senseless to the ground, never again to rise in human form. He dies, however, in triumph, believing he has reached the greatest of attainments: the knowledge of God's real name. When the flame of life departs from him, a candle in the synagogue burns out.

Such is the content of the first act. Khonnon, the tragic hero, meets his death just as he is about to rise to tragic proportions. This is not an artistic failure.

There is a belief among all the characters of the play, which none question, that there is a sympathetic understanding between the forces of nature and man, a belief that a continuity exists in the processes of nature which allows no sharp dividing line between life and death, will and fact, reality and imagination. There is no "life" and "death," as we ordinarily understand these terms, in the world of this drama. There are only transformations, transmigrations, and ascensions. Nothing is lost; it is only transformed. If Khonnon disappears from the scene, we are almost certain to see his immediate return.

* * *

The second act opens on a scene in a graveyard with a gravestone which carries the inscription: "Here lie a pure and holy bride and groom, murdered to the glory of God in the year 5408 [1648]. May their souls be bound to the living forever." This pair was murdered, we discover, before their marriage was consummated. This opening is a grim forecast of what is to come. Yet the scene is not harsh, for it suits the temper of the world in which these people move. The murdered pair is not really dead, for nothing dies in this world; and in a symbolic act of kindness, Laia invites them to the wedding.

22

Laia, who is the dominant character of the second act, has not remained unaffected by the events of the past few months. She appears to be in a trance—a fact attributed by the others to the busy preparations and festivities, but which is really the result of the presence of Khonnon which hovers over her being. She goes to the cemetery to invite her mother to the wedding. She cannot bypass the grave of Khonnon. When she returns she is a much changed person. When the groom approaches her with the wedding veil, she tears it away from him and thrusts it aside, crying out: "You are not my bridegroom." She rushes to the grave of the murdered pair, and here from her mouth there issues a cry, not her own, which proclaims: "I have returned to my predestined bride and I shall not leave her." The Messenger identifies the phenomenon as a dybbuk, and the curtain falls.

Dybbuk is derived from a Hebrew word meaning "attachment"; in kabbalistic lore it designates a migrant soul that attaches itself to the body of a living person and inhabits it. It can be exorcised only by a prescribed religious rite. A soul which has not been able to fulfill its function in its lifetime, according to the doctrine, is given another

opportunity to do so by being sent down to earth again in the form of a dybbuk. The dybbuk myth was an early and primitive attempt to give expression to the sense of justice and balance that man reads into the universe. In this drama the balance of justice has been disturbed and must be reestablished. A great human love has failed and Heaven has stepped in. The more pertinent reason for Heaven's intervention is, as yet, not given. How the people of the drama will deal with the dybbuk, this intruder, is the subject of the two concluding acts of the play.

The dybbuk is, of course, a representative of Khonnon, the tragic hero of the first act. But he is much more than that. He is the connecting link, so to speak, between the two worlds. The characters of the drama accept him, not as a psychological phenomenon, but as a metaphysical one. To them, the dybbuk is another aspect of reality and a further proof of the inherent harmony of the universe. But, above all, he is a terrible reminder that the human order had sinned against nature by being untrue to her, and that the supernatural has entered to restore the balance.

* * *

The third act takes place in the house of a Hassidic

24

rebbe or sage. Regarded as favorites of the Divine,
these saintly people were thought to possess magical
powers. When, however, the rebbe is confronted
with the hysterical Laia, he finds that his authority
alone is insufficient to drive out the dybbuk. He
summons a *minyen* (a quorum of ten Jews,
symbolically representative of the people of Israel,
who are required to recite prayers in the synagogue)
and attempts the exorcism on the strength of this
added authority. This fails, too. As a last resort, he
makes preparations to use his power of excommunication. White shrouds are donned, seven black
candles are lit, and seven rams' horns and seven
Scrolls are brought out. The Chief Rabbi of the city
is called on to grant permission for the proceedings.

At this point the people of this drama no longer
appear as mere playthings of their own imagination.
They are faced with an irrational force that refuses
to bend to their will. No longer are they at ease in
this universe. The rebbe himself appears troubled—
not that he doubts his power, but that he finds it
necessary to question his knowledge. There must be
greater significance to the dybbuk's stubborn
attachment to Laia than is immediately apparent.
And so there is, for when the Chief Rabbi arrives he
tells the gathering that he has had a dream in which

the father of Khonnon, long since dead, demanded that Sender, the father of Laia, be called to trial before the rabbinical court. A pact between the two men had been made years ago and broken by Sender. Its nature will be revealed at the trial.

* * *

The fourth act opens with an incantation against evil dreams—a traditional Hebrew prayer recited by the observant Jew on the occasion of a bad dream. The trial between the quick and the dead is made ready. A circle is drawn, a partition hung up, and the spirit of the dead man is invited to enter the courtroom. When all is ready, the spirit begins his tale: Sender and he were once fellow students and great friends. They shared each other's hopes and dreams; their destinies seemed entwined. Within a short interval of one another, they were each married. To consolidate their friendship, they vowed that their children would be united in marriage. The spirit recounts that his wife gave birth to a boy, Khonnon, and Sender's to a girl, Laia. It seemed as if God himself had given his approval to this solemn pact. But he died soon after his son was born and not much later the boy was entirely orphaned. Time passed as he watched Sender go his own way, failing to recognize the solemnly sworn oath. Sender failed in his obligations and with this failure brought about the death of the

spirit's only son. There is now not a soul left to say *Kaddish* (the prayer for the dead recited by the son in memory of his father) in his memory. He seeks justice from the earthly court.

Sender is of course guilty of a grave error, but how is justice to be realized? How can one repair the past? The court ponders the matter at great length and finally takes recourse in the Talmud—that very tome of learning Khonnon rejected—and delivers its verdict. It is this: Since it is not known whether, at the time the agreement between the two men was made, their wives had already conceived; and whereas no agreement which involves anything not yet in existence can be held valid, this agreement was therefore not binding on Sender. But since in the Upper World it was accepted as valid, and since Sender's subsequent action brought disaster upon his friend's family, Sender must give half his fortune to the poor and for the balance of his life light a memorial candle for Khonnon and his father.

This attempt to readjust the cosmic scales proves artificial and unsatisfactory. The world has been thrown into chaos, and the irrational refuses to be persuaded by the rational. When the spirit of the dead man is asked whether it complies with the

judgment, no answer is forthcoming. The judges are disturbed by this silence. When the dybbuk is asked to depart from the body of Laia, he refuses.

There is nothing left for the rebbe to do but to use his arbitrary power of excommunication. The shrouds, candles, rams' horns, and Scrolls are brought in and the anathema is pronounced. A great struggle ensues, and the dybbuk succumbs. Sender says *Kaddish* for the father and the son.

In order to forestall what seems about to happen, the rebbe demands that the wedding ceremony be performed immediately. But there are some delays and he becomes greatly agitated. He senses the disharmony, the injustice, and the tragedy. He traces a circle round Laia and departs. The soft, mystic chant heard at the beginning of the play rises again from the stage as Khonnon's image is seen reflected against the wall. Laia breaks out of the protective circle and approaches Khonnon. Their two forms merge into one.

* * *

Such is the nature of this drama. Its highly primitive, passionate movements break all bounds and barriers in its realization of the tragic. The human element as represented by Khonnon and Laia, the two tragic

heroes, is submerged in the great fall, but rises again, triumphantly, at the close. The immortal conflict that raged in the souls of these two protagonists, the conflict between dream and reality, emotion and reason, broke the heart in a thousand pieces, only to be reassembled again when the curtain was already beginning to fall.

This great conflict was not confined solely to the major characters. The drama as a whole is concerned with this highly significant theme. It is difficult to say where Ansky's sympathies lie—whether in the intense emotional states represented by Hassidism, which acts as a background to the whole drama and even threatens to destroy the limits of the art medium, or in the highly intellectual attempts, although orthodox and traditional, to regulate the life and movement of the characters caught in this tragic struggle against life. Perhaps it is enough to say that the unsuccessful resolution of this over-powering conflict is not confined solely to the elevation of the theater that ends when the curtain falls; but rather, that the struggle portrayed is like a symphonic poem whose echoes enter our dreams and disturb our nights.

SME

The Characters

The Dybbuk was performed for the first time in Warsaw, Poland, August 12, 1920, by the Vilna Troup under the direction of David Herman.

REB* SENDER OF BRINNITS
LAIA, *his daughter*
FRADEH, *her aged nanny*
GITTEL ⎱ LAIA'S *friends*
BASSIA ⎰
MENASHEH, LAIA'S *bridegroom*
NAKHMAN, *his father*
REB MENDEL, MENASHEH'S *tutor*
THE MESSENGER

*A title of address, like Mr., used always however with the first name. Not to be confused with *Rebbe* (used in the sense of Master or Teacher) or *Rabbi* (the title of ordination).

REB AZRIELKEH OF MIROPOLYE, *a* Tsaddik
    (a saintly man, holy man or sage)
MIKHOL, *his* gabbai *(attendant)*
REB SHIMSHON, *the Rabbi of Miropolye*
FIRST JUDGE
SECOND JUDGE
MEYER, shammes *(sexton) of the synagogue in Brinnits*
KHONNON
HENNAKH ⎰ *students at the* yeshiva *(talmudic academy)*
ASHER   ⎱   *in Brinnits*
FIRST BATLON**
SECOND BATLON ⎱ BATLONIM
THIRD BATLON
FIRST HASSID
SECOND HASSID ⎱ HASSIDIM
THIRD HASSID
AN ELDERLY WOMAN
A WEDDING GUEST *(invited, by custom, because he is*
    a stranger)
PAUPERS:
    A HUNCHBACK ⎱ men
    A MAN ON CRUTCHES

**Batlon* (pl. *batlonim*): a professional student who lives off the community, devoting himself to study and prayer—hence, also, an idler and daydreamer.

A WOMAN WITH A LIMP
A WOMAN WITH ONE ARM } old women
A BLIND WOMAN

A TALL PALE WOMAN
A WOMAN CARRYING A CHILD } young women

HASSIDIM, YESHIVA STUDENTS, HOUSEHOLDERS, SHOPKEEPERS, WEDDING GUESTS, PAUPERS, CHILDREN.

The first and second acts take place in Brinnits, the third and fourth in Miropolye. Three months elapse between the first and second acts; three days between the second and third; half a day between the third and fourth.

The melody of the opening and closing song as it was sung in Vitebsk, Ansky's birthplace.

MODERATO RELIGIOSO

Act One

 n the complete darkness of the theater, before the curtain goes up, a low mystic chant is heard, as if coming from afar.

> *Wherefore, O wherefore*
> *Has the soul*
> *Fallen from exalted heights*
> *To profoundest depths?*
> *Within itself, the fall*
> *Contains the ascension...*

The curtain rises slowly, disclosing an ancient wooden synagogue, its walls blackened by age, the ceiling supported by two wooden posts. From the

37

middle of the ceiling, directly over the *beema*,*
hangs an old brass chandelier. The table on the
beema is covered with a dark cloth. High up on the
rear center wall, small windows open into the
women's gallery. Along this wall stands a long bench
and in front of it a long wooden table which is
cluttered with books. Two tallow candle ends set in
small clay candlesticks are burning on the table.
They appear diminished beside the heaped-up
volumes. To the left of the bench and table, a
narrow door opens into a private study. In the
corner stands a bookcase. At the right wall, in the
middle, is the Holy Ark; to the left of this is the
cantor's reading stand on which a thick wax
memorial candle is burning. On both sides of the
Holy Ark are two windows. Benches span the entire
length of the wall and in front of them stand several
reading stands. At the left wall stands a large tile
oven, and near it, a bench. Alongside the bench a
table, also cluttered with books. A wash basin juts
out from the wall and a towel hangs from a ring. A
wide door leads out into the street and past it a
chest, above which, in a niche, a Perpetual Light is
burning.

---

*BEEMA IS THE RAILED DAIS IN THE MIDDLE OF THE SYNAGOGUE WHERE THE TORAH
IS READ.

At a reading stand, near the cantor's desk, sits
Hennakh, deeply engrossed in a book. Around the
table at the rear wall are five or six yeshiva students,
reclining in attitudes of weariness, studying the
Talmud to the tune of some dreamy, melancholy
melody. At the *beema*, MEYER, bent over, is busy
sorting the bags containing prayer shawls and
phylacteries. Around the table at the left wall sit
FIRST, SECOND, and THIRD BATLONIM: their eyes
sparkling and totally wrapt in dreams, they pass
their time in chanting. On the bench. near the oven,
THE MESSENGER lies outstretched, using his sack for a
pillow. At the bookcase stands KHONNON, his hand
resting on the top shelf, deeply lost in thought. It is
evening. A mystic atmosphere surrounds the
synagogue. Shadows lurk in the corners.

The three BATLONIM finish the chant "Wherefore"
and remain silent. A long pause ensues. Wrapt in
dreams all three sit motionless at the table.

FIRST BATLON (*as if relating a tale*): Reb Dovidl of
   Talna, may his merits protect us, had a golden
   chair on which was carved: "David, King of
   Israel, lives forever." (*Pause.*)

SECOND BATLON (*in the same tone*): Reb Israel of

39

Ruzhin, of blessed memory, carried himself like a true monarch. An orchestra of twenty-four musicians always played as he sat at table, and he never traveled with fewer than six horses in tandem.

THIRD BATLON (*enthusiastically*): And it's told of Reb Shmuel of Kaminka that he walked around in golden slippers. (*Rapturously.*) In *golden* slippers!

MESSENGER (*rises, and sitting on the bench, begins to speak in a low, soft voice as from afar*): The holy Reb Zusye of Annipol was a poor man all his days. He begged for alms and wore a peasant shirt girdled with a rope. Nevertheless, he accomplished no less than the Talna rebbe or the rebbe of Ruzhin.

FIRST BATLON (*annoyed*): You...don't be offended, but you don't know what's being discussed and you butt in anyway! When we speak of the greatness of the Talna rebbe and the Ruzhiner rebbe, do you really think it's their wealth we're talking about? Are there so few rich people in the world? It must be understood that both in the golden chair and in the orchestra,

42

and in the golden slippers as well, lies a deep secret of profoundest significance.

THIRD BATLON: Of course! Everyone knows that!

SECOND BATLON: Whose eyes were open saw it. It is told that when the Rabbi of Apt first encountered the Ruzhiner on the road, he threw himself to the ground to kiss the wheels of his carriage. When asked the significance of the deed, he cried out: "Fools! Don't you see that this is the chariot of the Lord!"

THIRD BATLÓN (*enraptured*): Ei-ei-ei!

FIRST BATLON: The substance of it all, then, lies in that the golden chair was actually not a chair at all, the orchestra, no orchestra, and the horses were no horses. They were all just imaginary, a reflection, serving only as the proper cloak and setting for greatness.

MESSENGER: True greatness needs no beautiful cloaks.

FIRST BATLON: You are mistaken. True greatness must have a fitting garb...

SECOND BATLON (*shrugging his shoulders*): Their

greatness! Their power! Are they to be measured?

FIRST BATLON: Their might is extraordinary! Did you ever hear the story of Reb Shmelke of Nickelsberg's whip? It's worth hearing. Once Reb Shmelke was called upon to settle a dispute between a poor man and a rich and powerful one before whom all had cause to tremble. Reb Shmelke heard both sides of the case and rendered his decision in favor of the poor man. The rich man became angry and declared that he would not abide by the decision. Calmly Reb Shmelke replied: "You will do as I say. When a rabbi renders a decision, it must be obeyed." The rich man lost his temper and began to shout: "I don't care a hoot for you or your decisions." At which Reb Shmelke drew himself up to his full height and cried out: "Carry out my decision this very instant! If not—I shall resort to my whip!" Now the rich man lost control of himself utterly and showered a torrent of insults upon the rabbi. Hearing this, Reb Shmelke slowly opened a drawer of his desk and, suddenly, out jumped the Original Serpent and coiled itself around the rich man's neck. Oh, what went on then! If you could have wit-

44

nessed the scene that followed! The rich man cried and shouted: "Help, help, Rebbe, forgive me, I shall do everything you say—only call off the Serpent." Reb Shmelke replied: "Tell your children and your children's children to obey the rebbe and fear his whip." Then he removed the Serpent.

THIRD BATLON: Ha, ha, ha. That's what I call a whip. (*Pause.*)

SECOND BATLON (*to the first*): I think you must have made a mistake. The story couldn't have happened with the Original Serpent.

THIRD BATLON: Really? Why Not?

SECOND BATLON: It's really quite simple. Reb Shmelke of Nickelsberg would have had nothing to do with the Original Serpent. The Original Serpent is, after all, the Evil One himself—Satan—Heaven protect us. (*Spits.*)

THIRD BATLON: Well, that's that. Reb Shmelke must have known what he was doing.

FIRST BATLON (*insulted*): I don't understand you. I tell you a story that took place before one and all; *dozens* of people saw it with their own eyes,

and you come along and say it couldn't have happened. As if I were speaking nonsense!

SECOND BATLON: God forbid, it's just that I thought that there were no such spells or signs with which one can summon the Evil One. (*Spits.*)

MESSENGER: The Devil can only be summoned by the utterance of the great, twofold Name of God, which can weld together in its flame the loftiest mountain peaks and the deepest valleys. (KHONNON *lifts his head and listens intently.*)

THIRD BATLON (*uneasy*): And is there no danger in speaking that Name?

MESSENGER (*meditatively*): A danger?...No. But through the spark's great yearning for the flame, the vessel might burst...

FIRST BATLON: There is a worker of wonders in my village, a wild miracle worker. For instance, he can light a fire with one spell and, with another, put it out. He can see what's happening a hundred miles away, and he can draw wine out of the wall merely by tapping it with his finger, et cetera. He told me himself that he knows spells that can create a golem, resurrect the dead, make him invisible, summon evil spirits...

even Satan himself. (*Spits.*) I heard it from his own mouth.

KHONNON (*who has all this time stood motionless and listened attentively to the discussion, now steps up to the table, looks first at* THE MESSENGER *and then at the* FIRST BATLON. *In a dreamy, distant voice*): Where is he?

(THE MESSENGER *fixes his gaze on* KHONNON *and watches him closely throughout.*)

FIRST BATLON (*surprised*): Who?

KHONNON: The worker of wonders.

FIRST BATLON: Where should he be! In my hometown, of course, if he is still alive.

KHONNON: Is it far from here?

FIRST BATLON: The village? Far! Very far; in the depths of Polesia.

KHONNON: How far?

FIRST BATLON: How far? A good month's journey, if not more... (*Pause.*) Why do you ask? Do you want to go to him? (KHONNON *remains silent.*) The name of the village is Krasna. The wonder worker's name is Elkhonnon.

KHONNON (*bemused, to himself*): Elkhonnon? El Khonnon?...The God of Khonnon?...

FIRST BATLON (*to the other* BATLONIM): I tell you he is a real miracle worker! Why, in broad daylight he once showed, using a spell...

SECOND BATLON (*interrupting*): That's enough about such things for one night! Especially in a holy place. Accidentally, someone might, God forbid blurt out one of those spells and then—disaster. It has happened before, God have mercy upon us. (KHONNON *walks out slowly. The others follow him with their eyes. Pause.*)

MESSENGER: Who is that young man?

FIRST BATLON: A yeshiva student (MEYER *closes the gates of the* beema *and walks up to the table.*)

SECOND BATLON: A priceless vessel, a genius.

THIRD BATLON: A brilliant mind! Five hundred pages of the Talmud at his fingertips, by memory.

MESSENGER: Where does he come from?

MEYER: He is from somewhere in Lithuania. Studied here at the yeshiva where he distinguished himself as the best student in the school. After being ordained a rabbi he suddenly disappeared, and

was not heard of for a whole year. It was said he went to lead a life of wandering in penance for the sins of our people. Not long ago he returned, no longer the young man we knew... constantly absorbed in his thoughts, fasting from Sabbath to Sabbath, continually performing ritual ablutions...(*Whispering.*) They also say that he meddles about with the Kabbala.

SECOND BATLON (*quietly*): The whole town is gossiping about it, too...He has already been asked for charms. He gives none, though...

THIRD BATLON: Who knows who he is. Perhaps one of the Great Ones. Who can tell? To spy on him might be dangerous...(*Pause.*)

SECOND BATLON (*yawning*): It's late...Time for bed. (*To the* FIRST BATLON, *smiling.*) It's a pity your miracle worker isn't here; the one who can draw wine out of the wall...I could certainly stand a little drink right now. I haven't had a bite all day!

FIRST BATLON: Today was almost like a fast-day for me too. I've had nothing to eat all day but a crust of bread after morning prayers.

Meyer (*secretly and gleefully*): You just wait. I have a feeling we'll be celebrating before long. Sender has gone off to inspect a bridegroom for his only daughter. Let's hope they come to some agreement, he'll provide us with a fine feast.

Second Batlon: Bah! I don't believe they'll come to an agreement. He's been out three times interviewing prospective bridegrooms and always returns alone. Either it's the young man who doesn't suit him, and if it's not the young man, it's the family, and if both are all right, it's the dowry. No one should be so choosy.

Meyer: Sender can afford to be choosy. He's rich, he comes from a fine family, and his only daughter has grown into a beautiful girl.

Third Batlon (*enthusiastically*): I like Sender! He is a real Hassid, one of the Miropolye Hassidim, full of that fire!...

First Batlon (*coldly*): He's a good Hassid, all right, no question of that. But he might have done something different in betrothing his only daughter.

Third Batlon: Why? What do you mean?

First Batlon: In the olden days, when a rich man,

especially from a fine family, wanted to marry off his daughter, he didn't look for money or pedigree; he went away to some famous yeshiva, made the head of the yeshiva a generous gift, and the rabbi would then chose the cream of the crop as a husband for the man's daughter. Sender could have done that, too.

MESSENGER: He might even have found a suitable bridegroom here, in this yeshiva.

FIRST BATLON (*surprised*): How do you know?

MESSENGER: I'm only supposing.

THIRD BATLON (*hurriedly*): Now, now, now, let's not speak evil of others, especially about our own people...Marriages are preordained, there's nothing you can do about them...

(*The street door is flung open and an elderly woman with two small children at her side rushes in.*)

ELDERLY WOMAN (*runs with the children to the Holy Ark, crying and weeping*): Ei-ei! Almighty God! Help me! Come children! We will open the Holy Ark, we will cling to the Holy Scrolls and not depart until our tears have wrought a cure for your mother. (*Opens the Holy Ark and*

51

buries her head among the Scrolls, intoning in a wailing voice.) God of Abraham, of Isaac, and of Jacob, behold my woe; behold the suffering of these little ones and do not take their mother from them in her youth. Holy Scrolls, intercede on behalf of a wretched widow! Holy Scrolls, beloved mothers, go—no run— to Almighty God, cry, beg, that the lovely young sapling be not torn out with its roots, that the little dove be not cast out of its nest, that the silent lamb be not taken from its flock ...(*Hysterically.*) I will tear worlds asunder, I will split the heavens! I will not leave this place until the crown of my head is restored to me!...

MEYER (*goes to her, touches her very gently, speaks softly*): Khannah-Esther, should I summon a *minyen* to recite the Psalms?

ELDERLY WOMAN (*withdraws her head from the Ark and looking at Meyer, uncomprehendingly; speaks hurriedly*): Yes, summon a *minyen* to come and pray. Yes, have them come. But hurry, hurry! Every second is precious. She has been lying, speechless, these two days struggling with death!

MEYER: This very instant. I'll have ten men here at

once. (*Pleading.*) But we must give them something for their trouble...They're poor people.

ELDERLY WOMAN (*searching in her pocket*): Here's a
gildin! But make sure they do it.

MEYER: A *gildin?*...that's only three *groshen* each...
not very much.

ELDERLY WOMAN (*not hearing him*): Come, children,
let us run to the other synagogues. (*Hurries
out with the children.*)

MESSENGER (*to the* THIRD BATLON): This morning an
old woman came into the synagogue and prayed
before the Holy Ark. Her daughter had been in
labor for two days and hadn't given birth. Now
another woman has come to pray before the
Ark for a daughter who has been struggling
with death for two days...

THIRD BATLON: Well, what of it?

MESSENGER (*absorbed*): When the soul of a person
not yet dead must enter a body not yet born, a
struggle takes place. If the ailing woman dies, a
child is born; if she recovers, the child is born
dead.

FIRST BATLON (*surprised*): Ei, ei, ei! How blind man

is! Unable to see what's happening before his very eyes.

MEYER (*goes to the table*): Well! See how the Lord above has provided? We'll recite the Psalms, have our drink, and God will have mercy and send the sick woman a full recovery.

FIRST BATLAN (*to the students sitting half asleep at the big table*): Hey, there! Boys! Who wants to say prayers for the sick? There is something for everyone who does. (*The students at the table get up.*) We will use the small study.

(*The* THREE BATLONIM, MEYER *and all the students, except* HENNAKH, *go into the small prayer room. The melancholy chant "Blessed is the man..." is soon heard coming from the room.* THE MESSENGER *remains seated at the small table, immobile, his eyes fixed on the Ark. A long pause.* KHONNON *enters.*)

KHONNON (*very weary, deep in thought, he walks aimlessly, toward the Ark. He notices that it is open and is overcome*): The Holy Ark open? Who can have opened it? For whom has it opened in the middle of the night? (*Looks into the Ark.*) Holy Scrolls...nestling together so devotedly, calmly, and silently. Yet, concealed in

them are all the mysteries and allusions, all the enigmas and miracles from the six days of creation to the end of all generations. And how difficult it is, how hard to wrest from them a single secret, a single clue! (*Counts the Scrolls.*) One, two, three, four, five, six, seven, eight, nine Scrolls. That's the word *emet*, "truth," according to the minor numerical system...And there are four handles on each Scroll, the four Trees of Life. Again, thirty-six! Not an hour passes that I don't stumble on that number. But what that means—I don't know. Yet I feel that in that number lies the essence...Laia's name comes to thirty-six. Thrice thirty-six—is Khonnon..."Laia" makes "Lai=a"—"not God" ...not through God...(*Shudders.*) What a terrible thought...how it entices and draws me to itself.

HENNAKH (*lifts his head, looks attentively at* KHON-NON): Khonnon. You always walk around as if you were in a daze.

KHONNON (*steps back from the Ark. He walks slowly to* HENNAKH, *and stands before him, deep in thought*): Secrets and clues without end, and the right path is not to be seen...(*short pause*). The name of the town is Krasna and the

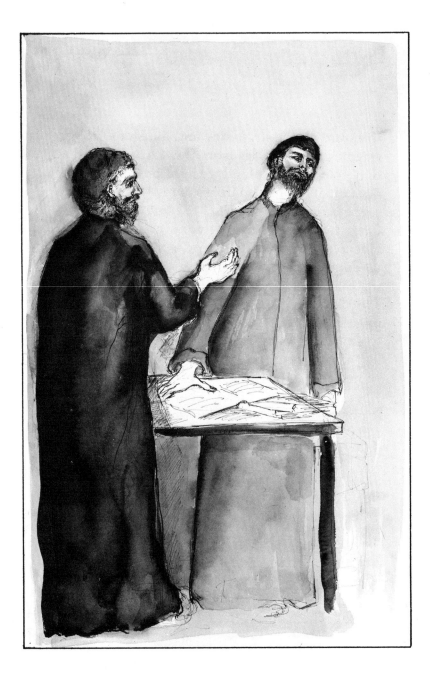

name of the miracle worker is Reb Elkhonnon...

HENNAKH: What's that you're saying?

KHONNON (*as if waking out of a trance*): I? Nothing ...I was just thinking...

HENNAKH (*shaking his head*): You've buried yourself too much in Kabbala, Khonnon...You haven't touched a book since you're back.

KHONNON (*not understanding*): Haven't touched a book? What book?

HENNAKH: What kind of question is that? The Talmud, the Laws, of course....

KHONNON (*still not out of his trance*): Talmud?... Laws?...I haven't touched them?...Talmud is cold and dry...Laws are cold and dry...(*Suddenly himself again, speaks excitedly.*) Beneath this earth is a world precisely like the world above. It has fields and forests, oceans and deserts, cities and villages. Over the fields and deserts rage violent high winds, on the oceans great vessels sail, and in the dense forests reigns eternal fear, and the thunder echoes...Only one thing is lacking. There is no vaulting sky from whence the fiery lightning can descend and the blinding sun can shine...It is the same with the

Talmud. Thus is the Talmud deep, vast, and glorious. But it chains one to the earth, not allowing you to soar to the heights. (*Ecstatically.*) But Kabbala! Kabbala. It tears the soul from the earth! It raises man to the highest summits and opens all the heavens before his eyes, it leads directly to Paradise, it reaches out to the infinite! It unravels the edge of the Great Curtain itself. (*Collapses.*) I have no strength...I feel faint...

HENNAKH (*very serious*): That's all true. But to attempt these heights is dangerous. You might lose your grip and plunge into the abyss. The Talmud raises the soul slowly onto the heights and protects it like a faithful sentinel who neither sleeps nor dreams. It seizes hold of a person with an iron grip that prevents him from turning aside from the straight path, either to the right or to the left. But the Kabbala... Remember what the Talmud says? (*Intones the following in the manner of talmudic recitation.*) "Four reached Paradise: Ben Azzay, Ben Zoma, Akhar, and Reb Akiva. Ben Azzay glanced in and lost his life. Ben Zoma looked within and lost his reason. Akhar renounced his

faith and became a heretic. Reb Akiva, alone, entered and left unharmed."

KHONNON: Don't try to frighten me with them. We don't know how they went in or with what. Perhaps they stumbled because they went out of curiosity and not to elevate themselves. We know that others went in after them—the holy Ari, the holy Baal Shem Tov. They did not fall.

HENNAKH: Are you comparing yourself to them?

KHONNON: I am not comparing myself to anyone. I go my own way.

HENNAKH: What way is that?

KHONNON: You wouldn't understand.

HENNAKH: I'll understand you. My soul also yearns for the higher planes.

KHONNON (*thinking a while*): The labor of our holy men consists in cleansing human souls, in stripping away the outer layers of sin, and in raising them back to their radiant source. This work is difficult because, as it is said, "sin hovers at the door." One soul is cleansed of its sins and another appears in its place, bespattered by more

sin. One generation of men is brought to repentance and another arrives, even more stiffnecked. As the generations of men become feebler and weaker, the sins become all the stronger—and our holy men, ever fewer.

HENNAKH: Well, according to your theory, what ought to be done?

KHONNON (*quietly, but with conviction*): It's not necessary to wage war against sin; one has only to refine it. As a goldsmith refines gold in a powerful flame, as a farmer winnows the grain from the chaff, so must sin be refined of its impurities so that nothing but holiness is left.

HENNAKH (*astonished*): Holiness in sin? How is that possible?

KHONNON: All things created by God have a spark of holiness.

HENNAKH: Sin was not created by God but by Satan.

KHONNON: And who created Satan? Is not Satan called the *sitreh-akhreh,* "the other side," meaning the other aspect of God? And if Satan is an aspect of God, he must have a spark of holiness in him.

HENNAKH (*crushed*): Holiness in Satan! I cannot...I don't understand it! Let me think. (*Lets his head drop into his arms which rest on the bookstand. Pause.*)

KHONNON (*goes up to* HENNAKH, *bends down to him and in a trembling voice*): Which sin is the most powerful? Which sin is the most difficult to overcome? The sin of lust for a woman, isn't that so?

HENNAKH (*without lifting his head*): Yes...

KHONNON: And when you refine this very sin in a powerful fire, the greatest of sins becomes the highest holiness; it becomes the Song of Songs. (*With bated breath.*) The Song of Songs! (*Straightens himself out and begins to sing in a rapturous, although subdued, voice.*) "Behold thou art fair, my predestined; behold thou art fair, thine eyes like doves gaze out from under thy brows, thy hair is as a flock of kids that scamper down Mount Gilead. Thy teeth are like a flock of sheep, even shorn, that have come up from the washing; whereof all are paired and none barren among them."

(MEYER *emerges from the prayer room. A soft knock is heard at the door which is opened hesitatingly and*

LAIA *enters, leading* FRADEH *by the hand.* GITTEL *follows. They remain standing near the door.*)

MEYER (*sees them, is very surprised, and welcomes them obsequiously*): Look! Reb Sender's daughter!...Laia!

LAIA (*embarrassed*): Remember? You promised to show me the old embroidered curtains for the Holy Ark.

(*As soon as her voice is heard,* KHONNON *cuts off his singing. He stares with wide open eyes at* LAIA *During the whole time she is in the synagogue he alternates between staring at her and standing with his eyes closed in ecstasy.*)

FRADEH: Show her the curtains, Meyerleh; the old ones, the most beautiful. Laialeh has promised to embroider one for the anniversary of her mother's death. She will embroider it with fine gold and on the best of velvet, the way they used to do it in the old days—with little lions and eagles. When they will hang it on the Holy Ark her mother's soul will rejoice in heaven.

(LAIA *looks around her uneasily. She notices* KHON-

NON *and lowers her eyes. She remains standing, tense, for the rest of the scene.*)

MEYER: Oh, with the greatest of pleasure. Why not! I'll bring them at once; the most beautiful, the oldest. (*Goes to the chest near the street door and takes out the curtains.*)

GITTEL (*grasping* LAIA's *hand*): Laia, aren't you a-fraid to be in the synagogue at night?

LAIA: I have never been in the synagogue at night... except on Simkhas Torah; that's a happy holi-day though, and the synagogue is bright and the people happy. But now...how gloomy every-thing seems—how sad!

FRADEH: A synogogue must be sad, my children. The dead come here at night to pray, and, when they depart, they leave their sorrows behind.

GITTEL: Granny, don't speak about the dead, it frightens me.

FRADEH (*not hearing her*): And every morning at daybreak, when the Almighty weeps over the destruction of the Temple, His holy tears fall in the synagogues. That's why the walls of old synagogues are tear-stained and it is forbidden

to whitewash them. If you try to, the walls become enraged and throw their stones in anger.

LAIA: How old this synagogue is; how very old! I never noticed that from the outside.

FRADEH: It's very, very old, my child. They even say it was found beneath the earth, already built. How many times was this place laid to waste, how many times was the city burned to ash—and only the synagogue was untouched. Once only, the roof caught fire, and innumerable doves came flocking down and with their little wings they fanned out the flames.

LAIA (*not hearing her, as though to herself*): How sad it is here and how loving! I feel I never want to leave this place. I want to fall against those tear-stained walls, embrace them wholeheartedly, and ask them why they are so sad and so pensive, so melancholy and silent. I wish...I don't know myself what I wish; I only know that my heart is torn with sorrow and pity.

MEYER (*brings the curtains to the* beema *and spreads one out*): This is the oldest one, more than two hundred years old. It's used only on Passover.

GITTEL (*delighted*): Look, Laialeh. How magnificent!

Two lions embroidered in heavy gold on stiff brown velvet. They are holding the star of David. On both sides are two trees with doves on them! You can't get such velvet nowadays, nor such gold.

LAIA: The curtain is so touching and so sad. (*Caresses and kisses it.*)

GITTEL (*takes hold of* LAIA's *hand, whispering*): Look, Laia. A young man standing over there is looking at you. How strangely he stares at you!

LAIA (*casting her eyes down even lower*): He's a yeshiva student...Khonnon...He used to eat at our house.

GITTEL: He stares at you as though he were calling you to him with his eyes. He'd like to come over, but he doesn't dare.

LAIA: I wonder why he's so pale and so sad. He must have been ill...

GITTEL: He's not sad; his eyes are sparkling.

LAIA: His eyes always sparkle. What eyes! When he speaks to me, he can hardly catch his breath. Me, too...After all, it isn't proper for a girl to speak to a strange young man...

FRADEH (*to* MEYER): Meyer, will you allow us to kiss the Holy Scrolls? It's wrong to be a guest in God's house and not kiss his holy Torah.

MEYER: Of course, of course. Let's go.

(*He leads the way, followed by* BITTEL *and* FRADEH, *and then* LAIA. MEYER *takes a Scroll from the Ark and gives it to* FRADEH *to kiss.*)

LAIA (*passing* KHONNON, *stops for a moment, and says softly*): Good evening, Khonnon. You have come back?

KHONNON (*breathless*): Yes.

FRADEH: Come Laialeh, let us kiss the Scroll.

(LAIA *goes up to the Holy Ark.* MEYER *holds the Scroll for her to kiss. She hugs it close to her and kisses it passionately.*)

FRADEH (*continuing*): Enough, my child; that'll do. It's forbidden to kiss a Scroll for too long. Scrolls are written with black fire upon white fire. (*Suddenly becoming alarmed.*) Oh, it's late; it's so late. Let's go home, children; come, quickly!

(*They rush out.* MEYER *closes the Ark and follows them out.*)

KHONNON (*stands a while, his eyes closed, and then resumes singing the Song of Songs from where he had left off*): "Thy lips are like a thread of scarlet, and thy mouth is comely; thy temples are like pomegranates beneath thy bridal veil."

HENNAKH (*lifts up his head and looks at* KHONNON): Khonnon, what are you singing?

(KHONNON *stops singing, opens his eyes, looks at* HENNAKH.)

HENNAKH (*continuing*): Your earlocks are wet. Have you been to the ritual bath again?

KHONNON: Yes.

HENNAKH: When you perform the rites at the *mikvah*, do you recite incantations? Do you follow those prescribed in the *Book of Razial*?

KHONNON: Yes.

HENNAKH: And you are not afraid?

KHONNON: No.

sion. MEYER *enters from the street; the* FIRST BATLON *comes in from the prayer room.*)

FIRST BATLON: Recited eighteen Psalms and that's enough. What does she expect; all of them for a *gildin?* You go talk to them—once they start reciting, they go on and on.

(ASHER *runs in, excited.*)

ASHER: Just met Borukh the tailor. He's come back from Klimovka where Sender's been trying to come to terms with the bridegroom's family. The whole thing's fallen through. Sender wanted the bridegroom's family to board the couple for ten years; they only agreed to five— so they parted.

MEYER: That's the fourth time!

THIRD BATLON: What heartbreak!

MESSENGER (*to the* THIRD BATLON *with a smile*): You said yourself, just a little while ago, that marriages are preordained.

HENNAKH: And you fast all week, from Sabbath to Sabbath? Isn't it hard?

KHONNON: It is harder for me to eat on the Sabbath

than to fast all week. I have lost all desire for food. (*Pause.*)

HENNAKH (*intimately*): Why are you doing this? What are you trying to attain?

KHONNON (*as though to himself*): I want...I want to attain a clear and sparkling diamond, dissolve it with tears, and absorb it into my soul...I want to attain to the rays of the third plane, to the rays of the third sphere, the sphere of beauty...I want...(*Suddenly agitated.*) Yes! I must still get two barrels of gold coins...for one who can count only coins.

HENNAKH (*astonished*): What! Be careful, Khonnon; you are at the edge of a slippery path. Not by holy powers will you attain to these things.

KHONNON (*looks at him defiantly*): What if not by holy means? And not through holy powers?

HENNAKH (*very frightened*): I'm afraid to speak to you, afraid to be near you. (*Goes out quickly.*)

(KHONNON *remains motionless with a defiant expres-*

KHONNON (*straightens up and cries out with rapture*): Another victory! (*Falls back limp on the bench and remains sitting with a blissful expression on his face.*)

MESSENGER (*takes his sack and removes a lantern*): It's time to be on my way.

MEYER: What's your hurry?

MESSENGER: I am a messenger. Important people employ me to bring them urgent news and rare objects. I must hurry. The time is not my own.

MEYER: But at least you'll wait until daybreak.

MESSENGER: Until daybreak is a long way off and my road is long. I'll leave around midnight.

MEYER: It's pitch dark outside.

MESSENGER: With my lantern I shan't go astray.

(*The* SECOND *and* THIRD BATLONIM *and the yeshiva students come out of the prayer room.*)

SECOND BATLON: *Mazel tov!* May the Lord restore the sick woman to health.

ALL: Amen!

FIRST BATLON: We should buy some brandy and cake with the *gildin.*

MEYER: I've already done that. (*Removes a bottle and cake from under his coat.*) Come, let's drink a toast.

(*The door opens and* SENDER *walks in, coat unbuttoned, his hat pushed back. He is very happy. Three or four men follow him in.*)

MEYER and the BATLONIM (*together*): Oh, Reb Sender! Welcome!

SENDER: I was just driving by the synagogue—then I think to myself, I must look in and see what our people are doing. (*Notices the bottle in* MEYER'S *hand.*) I expected to find them sitting and studying or discussing profound ideas. Instead, they're about to have a little celebration. Ha, ha! True Miropolye Hassidim!

FIRST BATLON: Will you join us, Reb Sender?

SENDER: Dummy! The refreshments are on me! Wish me *mazel tov*. It's a lucky hour for me, my daughter is betrothed.

(KHONNON *springs up, shattered.*)

ALL: *Mazel tov! Mazel tov!*

MEYER: Someone told us just now that you couldn't come to terms with the family and that the whole thing fell through.

72

THIRD BATLON: We were sorry to hear it!

SENDER: It almost did, but at the last moment the bridegroom's family gave in and we signed the agreement.

KHONNON: Betrothed?...Betrothed? How's that possible? How can that be? (*In great despair.*) It was all in vain—nothing helped, neither the fasts, nor the ablutions, nor the spells, nor the incantations. All useless?...Now, what? Where can I turn? What can I do?...(*Clutches at his breast and straightens up. His face assumes an ecstatic expression..*) Ah—ah—ah! At last the secret of the great twofold Name is revealed before my eyes. I...I have won...won! (*Falls to the ground.*)

MESSENGER (*opens his lantern*): The light has gone out. A new one must be lit.

(*There is a frightening pause.*)

SENDER: Meyer, why is it so dark here? Let's have some light.

(MEYER *lights another candle.*)

MESSENGER (*goes quietly over to* SENDER): Have you come to terms with the family?

SENDER (*looks at him, surprised and a bit frightened*): Yes.

MESSENGER: It can happen that parents give their word and then break it. Sometimes a trial may be necessary. One must be very careful in these matters.

SENDER (*frightened, to* MEYER): Who is that man? I don't know him.

MEYER: He's a stranger, a messenger.

SENDER: What does he want of me?

MEYER: I don't know.

SENDER (*calming down*): Asher, hop over to my house and have them prepare some drinks, preserves, and something good to eat. Put a move on!

(ASHER *runs out.*)

SENDER (*continuing*): We might as well sit around here while they're getting ready. Anyone hear a new saying of our rebbe's? A parable, a new

wonder? Every gesture of his is more precious than jewels.

FIRST BATLON (*to* MEYER): Save the bottle; we'll have it tomorrow.

(MEYER *puts it away.*)

MESSENGER: I will recount one of his parables. A very wealthy but miserly Hassid once paid a visit to the rebbe. The rebbe took him by the hand, led him to a window and said: "Take a look!" The wealthy man looked through the window out onto the street. "What do you see?" the rebbe asked him. The wealthy man answered: "I see people." The rebbe then took the wealthy man and led him to a mirror and said, "Take a look. What do you see now?" "Now I see myself," answered the rich man. Then the rebbe said: "Pay attention, now. There is glass in the window and there is glass in the mirror. But the glass in the mirror is covered with a little silver, and as soon as the glass is silvered you cease to see others and see only yourself."

THIRD BATLON: Oh, oh, oh! Sweeter than honey!

FIRST BATLON: Holy words!...

SENDER (*to the* MESSENGER): Hey! What? Are you trying to needle me?

MESSENGER: God forbid!

SECOND BATLON: Let's have a song. (*To the* THIRD BATLON.) Sing the rebbe's melody.

(*The* THIRD BATLON *begins to intone a low, mystic Hassidic melody. The others join in.*)

SENDER (*abruptly, rising from his seat*): Now, a dance! Is Sender going to marry off his only daughter without a little dancing? What kind of Miropolye Hassidim would we be!

(SENDER, *the* BATLONIM *and* MEYER *put their arms around each other's shoulders, make a circle, and turn their eyes to heaven; slowly they circle around one spot to the sound of a monotonous, mystic melody; their eyes sparkle.* SENDER *breaks away from the circle joyfully.*)

SENDER (*continuing*): Now a merry dance! Come on, everyone!

SECOND BATLON: Hey there, boys! Everybody, over here!

(*Several of the* STUDENTS *join in.*)

SECOND BATLON (*continuing*): Hennakh! Khonnon! Where are you? Over here! A merry dance!

SENDER (*a bit confused*): Ah, Khonnon. My Khonke is here, isn't he? Where is he? Bring him over here right now!

MEYER (*notices* KHONNON *on the floor*): Why, he's asleep on the floor!

SENDER: Wake him up! Wake him up!

MEYER (*tries to wake him, frightened*): He's not waking up!

(*All approach* KHONNON *and try to rouse him.*)

FIRST BATLON (*cries out in fright*): He's dead!

THIRD BATLON:A book fell from his hand. It's *The Angel Raziel!*

(*They are all shaken.*)

MESSENGER: He has been restored.

(*Curtain.*)

Act Two

A square in Brinnits. To the left, the old wooden synagogue; its architecture is very ancient. In front of the synagogue, a bit to the side, an old gravestone on a mound carries the inscription: "Here lie a pure and holy bride and groom, murdered to the glory of God in the year 5408. May their souls be bound to the living, forever." Past the synagogue, a small street, a few little houses that gradually merge into the backdrop.

On the right—SENDER's house. It is a frame structure with a large porch. Beyond the house, a wide gate opens into a courtyard through which is seen a little street with a row of small shops which gradually merge into the backdrop. On the backdrop, right

side, beyond the small shops, a tavern appears, then an imposing mansion and grounds. A wide pathway leads toward the river; its far side, high on the bank, is dotted with gravestones. To the left, a bridge spans the river, then a bathhouse, and, finally, a poorhouse. A forest appears in the far distance.

The gate to SENDER's courtyard is wide open. In the courtyard stand long tables which extend out into the square. The tables are laden with food, and around them sit beggars, cripples, old people, and children. They devour the food ravenously. Waiters carry large platters of food and baskets of bread from the house to the tables.

Women sit in front of the houses and shops, busy knitting. Their eyes are fixed on SENDER's house. Shopkeepers and students, carrying their prayer shawls and phylacteries, are seen coming out of the synagogue. Some go into the shops and houses; others stand about in groups, talking. Music, dancing, and loud talk is heard coming from the direction of SENDER's courtyard.

It is evening. In the middle of the street, in front of the synagogue, stands the WEDDING GUEST. He is an elderly man dressed in a satin kaftan and has his

hands tucked into his belt. Near him stands the Second Batlon.

GUEST (*examing the synagogue*): What a noble synagogue: beautiful, a fine structure, spacious. The Holy Spirit rests upon her. Looks quite old?

SECOND BATLON: Very old. Oldtimers say that even their grandfathers couldn't remember when it was built.

GUEST (*notices the gravestone*): And what is this? (*Goes closer and reads.*) "Here lie a holy and pure bride and groom, murdered to the glory of God in the year 5408." A bride and groom who died as martyrs for the sanctification of God's name?

SECOND BATLON: That murderer, Khmelnicki, may his name be erased forever, attacked this town with his Cossacks, killed half the Jewish population and murdered this pair as they were being led to the wedding canopy. They were buried on the very spot where they were murdered, both in one grave. Ever since then, the spot has been know as "the holy grave." (*Whispering, as though disclosing a secret.*) Whenever the Rabbi performs a marriage ceremony, he hears sighs coming from the grave...It has become a

custom with us to come here after every wedding and cheer up the murdered pair by dancing around their grave.

GUEST: That's a fine custom.

(MEYER *comes out of* SENDER's *courtyard and approaches them.*)

MEYER (*excitedly*): What a feast for the poor! Never in all my life have I seen anything like it!

GUEST: Naturally. Sender's marrying off his only daughter.

MEYER (*enthusiastically*): First, a piece of fish for everyone; then, two servings of roast fowl; and dessert, too! And brandy and cake before the meal. It must have cost a fortune—you can't imagine how much!

SECOND BATLON: Sender knows what he's up to. It's no problem if you skimp on an invited guest. Let him gripe and blow off steam. But it's really dangerous to be stingy with the poor. Who can tell whom a beggar's coat might be covering? Maybe just a beggar, but it could be a disguise for someone quite different—a *tzaddik*...maybe even one of the Thirty-Six Just Men.

MEYER: Why not the Prophet Elijah himself? He always appears in the guise of a beggar.

GUEST: The poor are not the only ones who should be treated with care. Who can tell who anyone is, who he was in a previous incarnation, and why he was sent into this world?

(*The* MESSENGER *enters from the left lane, his sack over his shoulders.*)

MEYER (*sees the* MESSENGER, *goes over to him*): *Sholem aleikhem.* You have returned to us?

MESSENGER: I have been sent here again.

MEYER: You come in a happy hour; we're celebrating a sumptuous wedding.

MESSENGER: The wedding is the talk of the whole countryside.

MEYER: Perhaps you passed the bridegroom's party on your way here? They are a little late.

MESSENGER: The bridegroom will come in plenty of time. (*Goes to the synagogue.*)

(*The* GUEST, *the* SECOND BATLON, *and* MEYER *go into the courtyard.* LAIA, *in her wedding gown, is seen*

behind the tables. She dances with one after another of the old pauper women. The others crowd around her. Those who have already danced with her go out into the square and stand about in small groups.)

OLD WOMAN WITH A CHILD (*contentedly*): I danced with the bride.

LAME WOMAN: Me, too. I put my arms around her and danced. Hee, hee.

HUNCHBACK: Why does the bride only dance with the women? I'd like to put *my* arms around her, too, and dance. Hee, hee, hee!

SEVERAL PAUPERS: Ha, ha, ha!

(FRADEH, GITTEL *and* BASSIA *come out onto the porch.*)

FRADEH (*uneasy*): Oh, for goodness' sake! Laia is still dancing with the poor folk. She must be getting dizzy by now. Children, go and bring her over here. (*Sits down on a bench.*)

(GITTEL *and* BASSIA *go to* LAIA.)

GITTEL: That's enough dancing. Come on, Laia.

84

BASSIA: You'll get dizzy. (*She and* GITTEL *take* LAIA *by the arms and try to lead her away.*)

THE PAUPER WOMEN (*surround* LAIA, *begging and whining*):
—She hasn't danced with me yet. I'm just as good as the others.
—I've waited a whole hour to dance with her!
—Let me. My turn comes after Elka.
—She's had about ten dances with that gimpy gossip and not even one with me. I never have any luck.

MEYER (*comes out of the yard and climbs onto a bench. In a high-pitched voice, he sings the following, in the manner of a jester*):

Come one, come all, come quickly to the door,
Your host desires to see you all.
Sender himself wll distribute the alms,
He'll put ten *groshen* in everyone's palms.

THE PAUPERS (*run quickly into the courtyard, pushing and shouting*): Ten *groshen!* Ten *groshen!*

(*The square is emptied of all people except* LAIA, GITTEL, BASSIA, *and an old* BLIND WOMAN.)

BLIND WOMAN (*seizes hold of* LAIA): I don't want the alms, just dance with me. Just one turn with me! It's been forty years since I last danced. Oh, how I danced in my youth! How I danced! (LAIA *takes the* OLD WOMAN *about the waist and dances with her. The* OLD WOMAN *doesn't let go of her. Begging*): More!...More!...(*They continue dancing. The* OLD WOMAN *runs short of breath and becomes hysterical*): More!... More!...

(GITTEL *drags the* OLD WOMAN *away to the courtyard and returns; together with* BASSIA, *they lead* LAIA *to the porch and sit down on a bench. The waiters and servants take away the tables and lock the gate.*)

FRADEH: Oh, Laia, you're as white as a sheet. You've worn yourself out, haven't you?

LAIA (*eyes closed, head thrown back, speaks as though in a dream*): They put their arms around me; crowded all about me; pushed themselves against me and clutched at me with their cold, dry fingers...My head began to swim, I grew faint...Then someone lifted me high up into the air and carried me far, far away...

BASSIA (*frightened*): Laia, look, see how they've

87

creased and stained your gown. What will you do now?

LAIA (*as before*): If the bride is left alone before the wedding, demons come and carry her off.

FRADEH (*frightened*): What are you talking about, Laia? You mustn't mention those dark spirits by name. They lie hidden and buried in every corner, in every hole and in every crevice. They see everything, and they hear everything, and they lie in wait for someone to call them by their unclean names. Then they leap out and throw themselves at you. Pfoo, pfoo, pfoo!

LAIA (*opens her eyes*): They are not evil...

FRADEH: You mustn't even believe them. If you believe, they run riot and do a lot of mischief...

LAIA (*with conviction*): Granny! We are not surrounded by evil spirits, but by the souls of people who died before their time. They are the ones who watch and listen to everything we do and say.

FRADEH: God be with us, child! What are you talking about? Souls? What souls? Clean, pure souls

soar up to Heaven and rest in the brightness of Paradise.

LAIA: No, Granny, they are here, with us. (*In another tone.*) Grandma, people are born to live long lives. So what happens to all the unlived years if they die before their time? What becomes of their joys and of their sorrows? To all the thoughts they had no chance to think? And to all the deeds they had no chance to perform? What happens to the children they had no chance to bring into the world? What happens to all of it? Where do you think it all goes? Where? (*Lost in thought.*) There once lived a young man with a lofty soul and profound thoughts. A long life lay ahead of him. And suddenly, in a single instant, his life was cut off and he was taken away and buried by strangers in a strange grave. (*Despondently.*) What's become of what was left of his life? His speech that was silenced; his prayers that were interrupted?...Grandma. When a candle is blown out, we light it and it's allowed to burn down to its very last flicker. Then how can the flame of an unfinished life be snuffed out forever? Is that possible?

FRADEH (*shaking her head*): My child, you mustn't

think about such things. The Lord above knows what He's doing. We are blind and we know nothing.

(*The* MESSENGER *comes up to them, unnoticed, and remains standing close behind them.*)

LAIA (*not hearing* FRADEH *and with conviction*): No, Granny, no one's life is ever lost completely. When someone dies before his time, his soul comes back to earth to live out his unlived years, complete his still unfinished deeds, and experience the joys and sorrows he had no time for in life. (*Pause.*) Grandma. Remember when you told us that at midnight the dead come to the synagogue to pray? They come to complete the prayers there was no time for them to say.

(*Pause.*) My mother died young and she didn't have a chance to live through everything she was meant to. That's why I'm going to the cemetery today to invite her to the wedding and ask her to join Father when he leads me to the wedding canopy. She'll come and she'll dance with me, too. It's like that with all the souls that depart the world before their time. They are here, among us, unseen and unfelt. (*In a low*

voice): Granny, whoever really wants to can see them and hear their voices and understand their thoughts...I know...(*Pause. Points to the grave.*) I've known this holy grave since I was a child. I know the bride and groom well who are buried there. I've seen them in my dreams and awake, many times. They are as dear to me as my own family...(*Deep in thought.*) They were so young and lovely when they walked to the canopy together. Before them lay a long life; a beautiful life. Suddenly, evil men with axes attacked them—and both fell dead. They were buried together in the same grave so that they would never be separated. Whenever there's a wedding and we dance around their grave, they leave the grave and partake of the happiness of the bride and groom...(*Rises and walks over to the grave.* FRADEH, GITTEL, *and* BASSIA *follow her. Lifts her arms and in a loud voice.*) Holy bride and groom! I invite you to my wedding! Come and stand near me under the canopy.

(*Lively march music is heard.* LAIA *cries out in fear and almost falls.*)

GITTEL (*catching* LAIA): What frightened you so?

93

That must be the groom arriving and they're greeting him as he comes into town.

BASSIA (*excited*): I'll run and take a peep at him.

GITTEL: Me, too. Then we'll come back and tell you what he's like. Right?

LAIA (*shaking her head*): No.

BASSIA: You're shy. Don't be shy, silly. We won't tell anyone.

(*They run off swiftly.* LAIA *and* FRADEH *return to the porch.*)

FRADEH: The bride always asks her friends to sneak a look at the groom and tell whether he is fair or dark.

MESSENGER (*coming up closer*): Bride!

LAIA (*trembles and turns toward him*): What is it? (*Looks intently at him.*)

MESSENGER: Souls of the departed do return to earth, but not as disembodied spirits. Some souls must pass through many physical incarnations before they are purified. (LAIA *listens with increasing attention.*) Souls that have sinned might be

transformed into birds or beasts or fish—even into plants. They're unable to purify themselves by their own efforts alone, but must await the coming of a holy sage to free them and cleanse them. Then there are those souls that enter the bodies of the newborn and cleanse themselves by their own efforts in performing good deeds.

LAIA (*in a trembling voice*): Yes...Yes...Go on...

MESSENGER: Then there are the homeless souls that can find no repose; they beguile their way into someone's living body as a *dybbuk*, through which they attain purification.

(*He disappears.* LAIA *remains standing, astonished.* SENDER *comes out of the house.*)

SENDER: Why are you sitting here, my child?

FRADEH: She wore herself out with the poor at their meal, and dancing with them afterwards. She's resting now.

SENDER: Oh! Bringing cheer to the poor—that's a pious thing to do. (*Looks at the sky.*) It's getting late. The bridegroom and his party are here. Are you ready?

FRADEH: She has still to go to the cemetery...

SENDER: Go, child, go to your mother's grave. (*Sighs.*) Weep over her grave and invite her to the wedding. Tell her that I want us both to lead our only daughter to the canopy. Tell her I have fulfilled all her dying wishes. I have devoted my entire life to you; brought you up to be a pure and virtuous daughter. And now I'm about to give you in marriage to a learned and God-fearing young man from a fine family. (*Wipes away his tears and, with bowed head, returns to the house. Pause.*)

LAIA: Granny, at the cemetery, may I invite others besides my mother?

FRADEH: Only close relatives. You should invite your grandfather, Reb Ephraim, and your Aunt Mireleh.

LAIA: I'd like to invite someone who's...not a relative.

FRADEH: That's forbidden, child. If you invite one stranger, the other dead might take offense and they can do a lot of mischief...

LAIA: Not exactly a stranger...He lived with us like one of the family.

FRADEH (*in a low voice, frightened*): Oh, dear child, that frightens me! I heard he died an unnatural

death. (LAIA *weeps quietly*.) There, there, don't cry; don't cry. Go ahead, invite him. I take the sin upon myself. (*Reminds herself.*) But I don't know where he's buried, and I don't like to ask.

LAIA: I know where he is.

FRADEH (*astonished*): How do you know?

LAIA: I saw his grave in a dream. (*Closes her eyes, deep in thought.*) I saw him too. And he told me about himself...and asked to be invited to the wedding.

(GITTEL *and* BASSIA *come running in.*)

GITTEL, BASSIA (*together, very excited*): We saw him! We saw him!

LAIA (*shaken*): Whom? Whom did you see?

GITTEL: Your bridegroom. He's dark, dark.

BASSIA: No, he's fair, he's fair.

GITTEL: Come, let's look at him again. (*Run off quickly.*)

LAIA (*rising*): Grandma, let's go to the cemetery.

FRADEH (*sadly*): All right, child...Oh, my, oh my!

(LAIA *puts a black shawl over her shoulders and exits with* FRADEH *by the lane on the right. The stage remains empty for a short while. Music is heard. Enter from the left lane,* NAKHMAN, REB MENDEL *and* MENASHE, *a short, emaciated youth who looks very frightened and stares about him with wide, questioning eyes; after them enter relatives, men and women, all dressed in holiday clothes.* SENDER *comes out to greet them.*)

SENDER (*shaking hands with* NAKHMAN): *Sholem aleikhem* and welcome! Welcome! (*They kiss. Shakes hands with* MENASHE *and kisses him. Shakes hands with the others.*) How was your journey, Nakhman?

NAKHMAN: We had a hard, miserable trip. First we missed the road and got lost in the fields. Then we blundered into a swamp and were nearly swallowed up in it. We almost didn't make it and I even had a feeling that evil spirits, God forbid, were mixed up in this somehow, to keep us from getting here. But, with God's help, as you see, we arrived in time.

SENDER: You must be very tired. You probably want to rest awhile.

NAKHMAN: There's no time for resting. We still have

so many details to work out in the marriage contract, the dowry, the expenses of the wedding, and so on...

SENDER: Of course. (*Puts his arm around* NAKHMAN *and they walk up and down the square, talking quietly.*)

REB MENDEL (*to* MENASHE): Remember! You're to sit still at the table. Don't fuss and keep your eyes lowered. And after the wedding feast, when the master of ceremonies calls out, "The bridegroom will now deliver his oration!" get right up, stand up on the bench, and begin in a loud voice and with the proper intonation. The louder, the better. And don't be bashful! Understand?

MENASHE (*mechanically*): I understand. (*Whispers.*) Rebbe, I am afraid.

REB MENDEL (*alarmed*): What are you afraid of? You didn't forget your speech, did you?

MENASHE: I remember the speech.

REB MENDEL: Then why are you afraid?

MENASHE (*in great anguish*): I don't know. I was terrified as soon as we left home. The places we rode through were all so strange to me, and

never in my life have I seen so many strange people. I'm frightened every time they look at me. I'm afraid of their eyes. (*Shudders.*) Rebbe! Nothing frightens me so much as strangers looking at me!

REB MENDEL: I'll charm the Evil Eye away from you.

MENASHE: Rebbe! I'd rather be left alone, I feel like hiding in some corner. Strangers keep crowding around me here from all sides. I have to talk with them, I have to answer their questions. I feel as though I were being led to the gallows. (*With mystic fright.*) Rebbe! Most of all I'm a-fraid of her...the girl...

REB MENDEL: Be brave. Try to control your fears, or else, God forbid, you might forget your oration. Come, let's go into the inn and go over it again. (*They start to leave.*)

MENASHE (*sees the gravestone, becomes frightened and clutches* REB MENDEL'*s hand*): Rebbe! Look at this! A grave in the middle of the street!!

(*They stop and read the inscription silently. Pause for a while and then, with downcast heads, go out through the lane on the left.* SENDER, NAKHMAN *and the relatives go into the house. The poor come out of*

SENDER'S *courtyard; with sacks over their shoulders and staffs in hand, they silently leave. Some pause a while in the square.*)

TALL PALE YOUNG WOMAN: Now the feast for the poor is over, too, just as though it never happened.

OLD WOMAN WITH A LIMP: There was supposed to be a plate of soup for everyone, but I didn't see any.

HUNCHBACK: And the pieces of *khale**** were so tiny.

MAN ON CRUTCHES: He's so rich! Would it have killed him to give each of us a whole loaf?

TALL PALE YOUNG WOMAN: They could have given us some chicken, too. Don't worry, the guests get chicken and goose and stuffed turkey...

BLIND OLD WOMAN: What's the difference? When we're dead, the worms will get it all. Oh my, oh my, oh my!

(*Go away slowly. The square remains empty for a moment. The* MESSENGER *walks slowly across the square and goes into the synagogue. Darkness begins*

*BRAIDED SABBATH BREAD.

to descend. The shopkeepers close their shops and leave. In the synagogue and in SENDER's *house, lights are lit.* SENDER, GITTEL *and* BASSIA *come out onto the porch and look around.*)

SENDER (*uneasy*): Where is Laia? Where's the old lady? Why aren't they back from the cemetery? I hope nothing has, God forbid, happened to them!

GITTEL, BASSIA: We'll go and meet them.

(LAIA *and* FRADEH *rush in from the lane on the right.*)

FRADEH: Hurry, hurry, child! Ei, we've been away so long! Why did I have to give in to you? I'm terrified that, God forbid, something dreadful may happen!

SENDER: Well. There you are. Why did you take so long?

(*Women come out of the house.*)

WOMEN: Bring the bride in to light the candles and say the blessings. (*They lead* LAIA *into the house.*)

FRADEH (*secretly to* GITTEL *and* BASSIA): She fainted. I

thought I'd never bring her round. I'm still shaky.

BASSIA: She's been fasting and it weakened her.

GITTEL: Did she cry a lot at her mother's grave?

FRADEH (*waving her hand*)? It's better not to ask what happened there...I'm trembling.

(*A chair is brought out and put near the door. LAIA is led out and is seated on the chair. Music plays as NAKHMAN, MENASHE, REB MENDEL, the relatives, enter from the left lane. MENASHE, carrying the bridal veil, approaches LAIA to cover her face with it. The MESSENGER comes out of the synagogue.*)

LAIA (*tears the veil from her face, jumps up, and pushing MENASHE away from her, cries out*): You are not my bridegroom!

(*There is a great commotion as everyone crowds around LAIA.*)

SENDER (*stunned*): Daughter! Laia, what's wrong?

LAIA (*tears herself away, runs to the grave and, spreading wide her arms*): Holy bride and groom, protect me! Save me! (*She falls. They*

104

run to her, lift her up. She looks wildly about and cries out, not in her own voice but in the voice of a man.) Ah-ah! You buried me! But I have returned to my destined bride and I shall not leave her! (NAKHMAN *goes over to* LAIA. *She shouts into his face.)* Murderer!

NAKHMAN *(trembling)*: She has gone mad.

MESSENGER: The bride has become possessed of a dybbuk.

(Curtain)

Act Three

In Miropolye, at the home of REB AZRIELKE, Grand Rabbi of Miropolye. A large room. To the right, a door leads to other rooms. Past the door stands a small Ark and reading stand. In front of these a small table, a sofa, several chairs. In the middle of the wall, rear, a door opens to the street. On both sides of this door are benches. Windows are above them. Left, a wide table covered with a white tablecloth spans almost the entire length of the wall. Pieces of *khale* for a blessing are piled up on the table. An armchair stands at the head of the table.

It is Sabbath evening after sundown. Hassidim stand around. MIKHOL, the Rabbi's attendant, is busy arranging and distributing the pieces of *khale*. The

107

MESSENGER sits near the Ark, surrounded by a group of Hassidim. Another group of Hassidim is busy studying. The FIRST and SECOND HASSIDIM stand in the middle of the room near the small table. From the inner rooms, the prayer, "God of Abraham, Isaac and Jacob" can be heard being chanted.

FIRST HASSID: The stranger's tales are fantastic. They can frighten you to death. I'm afraid to listen...

SECOND HASSID: Why?

FIRST HASSID: They are full of profound allusions... too difficult to grasp. I believe they have a flavor of the teachings of the Grand Rabbi of Bratslav...Who can tell?

SECOND HASSID: The older Hassidim are listening; why should we worry?

(*They join the group gathered round the* MESSENGER.)

THIRD HASSID: Tell another one!

MESSENGER: It's late. Time is short.

THIRD HASSID: It's not that late. The Rebbe won't be coming in for some time yet.

MESSENGER (*continues*): At world's end stands a high

108

mountain; on top of the mountain rests a great rock; and out of the rock flows a spring of clear water. At the other end of the world lies the heart of the world, for everything in the world has its heart and the whole world has a great heart. Now the heart of the world never takes its eyes from the clear spring of water, but gazes at it with insatiable longing—yearning and thirsting for the spring of clear water—but cannot take even the tiniest step in its direction. For the instant the heart makes a move from its place, it loses sight of the peak of the mountain with its clear spring; and, should the heart of the world lose sight of the clear spring, even for a single second, it loses its life's vitality and at the same time the world begins to die.

The clear spring is without time of its own and is only sustained by time that is granted it by the heart of the world. One day is all the heart allows it. When the day wanes, the clear spring begins to sing to the heart of the world, and the heart of the world to the clear spring. Their song spreads over the whole world and gleaming threads emerge from the song that reach out to the hearts of all things in the world and from one heart to another. And there is a man of

righteousness and grace who walks through the world and gathers these threads from the hearts and weaves them into time. When he has thus woven one day, he presents it to the heart of the world and the heart of the world presents it to the clear spring and the spring lives another day...

THIRD HASSID: The rebbe is coming!

(*Silence falls upon everyone. They all rise.* REB AZRIEKLE, *wearing a white kaftan and a fur-trimmed hat, enters through the door on the right. He is a very old man.* REB AZRIELKE *walks slowly to the table, weary and buried in thought, sinks heavily into the armchair.* MIKHOL *stands at his right. The Hassidim take their places around the table. The older among them sit on the benches; the younger ones stand behind them.* MIKHOL *distributes the* khale *among the Hassidim.*)

REB AZRIEKLE (*lifting up his head, begins to chant in a soft quavering voice*): "The feast of King David, the Messiah."

(*The others respond and say the blessing over the bread. They begin to sing quietly some sad, mystic*

110

melody. Pause. REB AZRIELKE *sighs deeply, rests his head on both hands and sits thus awhile, deep in thought. A heavy silence reigns over the entire room.* REB AZRIELKE *raises his head and begins to speak in a soft, trembling voice.*)

REB AZRIELKE: It is told of the holy Baal Shem, may his merits protect us. (*Short pause.*) There once came to Mezhibuzh a troupe of acrobats who performed in the streets. They stretched a rope across the width of the river, and one of them crossed the river on the tightrope. The whole town gathered to watch this marvelous feat. The holy Baal Shem also came down to the river and stood there along with the others, watching the man cross the river on the tightrope. This was a source of great amazement to his disciples, and they asked him to explain the significance of his coming out to watch such tricks. The holy Baal Shem answered them: "I came to see and observe how a man crosses a deep abyss. As I watched, I thought: Were man to devote as much energy to the discipline of his soul as this man had devoted to the discipline of his body, what deep chasms he could cross upon the slender cord of life!" (*Sighs deeply. Pause.*)

111

(*The* HASSIDIM *look at each other, enraptured.*)

FIRST HASSID: Magnificent!

SECOND HASSID: Marvel of marvels!

THIRD HASSID: Glorious!

REB AZRIELKE (*in a soft voice to* MIKHOL, *who bends down to him*): There is a stranger here.

MIKHOL (*looks about him*): He is a messenger and a student of the Kabbala, it appears.

REB AZRIELKE: What is his mission here?

MIKHOL: I don't know. Shall I ask him to leave?

REB AZRIELKE: God forbid. On the contrary, a stranger should be received with respect. Offer him a chair. (MIKHOL, *surprised, offers the* MESSENGER *a chair. No one notices it.* REB AZRIELKE *glances at one of the* HASSIDIM *who is singing a mystic melody. Pause.* REB AZRIELKE *now continues as before.*) God's world is great and holy. The holiest land in the world is the Land of Israel. In the Land of Israel, the holiest city is Jerusalem; in Jerusalem, the holiest spot was the Temple, and the holiest spot in the Temple was the Holy of Holies. (*Short pause.*) There are

seventy nations in the world. The holiest of
them is Israel. Within the nation of Israel, the
holiest tribe is the tribe of Levi; and in the tribe
of Levi, the holiest are the priests. Among the
priests, the holiest was the High Priest. (*Short
pause.*) There are 354 days in the year. The
holiest among them are the holidays. Holier
than these are the Sabbaths; and among the
Sabbaths, the holiest is the Day of Atonement,
the Sabbath of Sabbaths. (*Short pause.*) There
are seventy languages in the world. The holiest
language is Hebrew. Holiest of all things written
in this language is the Torah, and the holiest
portion of the Torah is the Ten Commandments. The holiest of all the words of the Ten
Commandments is the name of God.

(*Pause.*) And once a year, at the appointed hour,
these four most sacred holinesses of the world
encounter one another. This used to happen on
the Day of Atonement when the High Priest
entered the Holy of Holies and there uttered a-
loud the holy Name of God. And as this hour
was holy, so was it also full of danger both for
the High Priest and for the whole people of
Israel. For if, God forbid, during that hour a

sinful thought or desire had entered the mind of the High Priest, the world would have been destroyed. (*Pause.*) Every spot whereon a man may stand and lift his eyes to Heaven becomes a Holy of Holies; every man whom God has created in His image and in His likeness is a High Priest; every day of a man's life is a Day of Atonement; and every word that a man utters with his whole heart is the Name of God.

Therefore, a man's every sin and every injustice brings destruction upon the world. (*With a trembling voice.*) The human soul is ever drawn like a child to its mother's breast, through great pain and grief and through many incarnations, to reach its source, the Exalted Throne on High. But it sometimes happens that even after a soul has reached exalted heights, it is suddenly, God forbid, overwhelmed by evil, so that it stumbles and falls. And the higher the heights it attained, the deeper is its fall. With the fall of such a soul, the world is plunged in ruin, darkness descends on all holy places, and all ten spheres of creation mourn. (*Pause. As though suddenly awakening.*) My children! We will shorten our feast of farewell to the Sabbath today.

(*All, except* MIKHOL, *silently leave the room, deeply stired by what they heard. Short pause.*)

MIKHOL (*goes over to the table, timidly*): Rebbe. (REB AZRIELKE, *weary and sad, looks up at him.*) Reb Sender of Brinnits is here.

REB AZRIELKE (*mechanically repeating*): Sender of Brinnits. I know.

MIKHOL: A terrible calamity has befallen him. His daughter has become possessed of a dybbuk, God have mercy on us.

REB AZRIELKE: Possessed of a dybbuk. I know.

MIKHOL: He has brought her to you.

REB AZRIELKE (*as though to himself*): To me? To me? How can he come to me when there is no "me" to come to?...

MIKHOL: Rebbe, all the world comes to you.

REB AZRIELKE: All the world. A blind world. Blind sheep following a blind shepherd. If they were not blind, they would not come to me but to Him who *can* justly say "I," the only "I" in the world.

115

MIKHOL: Rebbe, you are His messenger.

REB AZRIELKE: That's what the world says, but I don't know...I've been sitting in the rebbe's chair for forty years now, and I'm still not sure I'm a messenger of God, praised be He. There are times when I do feel close to the All-Encompassing; I have no doubts then; I feel the power in me extending to the worlds above. But there are times when I lose that sure confidence. Then I am just as small and as weak as a little child. Then I need help myself.

MIKHOL: Rebbe, I remember once you came to me in the middle of the night and asked me to recite the Psalms with you. We recited them all night long, weeping together.

REB AZRIELKE: That was then. Now it is even worse. (*With a trembling voice.*) What do they want of me? I am old and weak. My body needs rest and my soul longs for solitude. Yet all the pain and anguish of the world is drawn to me. Each plea pierces my body like sharp needles. I have no strength left...I cannot!...

MIKHOL (*frightened*): Rebbe!

REB AZRIELKE (*sobbing*): I cannot go on!...I cannot!...

MIKHOL: Rebbe! Don't forget the generations of holy and righteous men of God who stand behind you. Your father, Reb Itchele, of blessed memory; your grandfather, the renowned scholar Reb Velvele the Great, who was a pupil of the Baal Shem...

REB AZRIELKE (*recovers, lifts his head*): My forebears...my saintly father who thrice had a revelation from Elijah...my uncle, Reb Meyer Ber, who could ascend to Heaven with the prayer "Hear O Israel"; my grandfather, the great Reb Velvele who could resurrect the dead. (*Turns toward* MIKHOL. *Vivaciously.*) Do you know, Mikhol, that my grandfather, the great Reb Velvele, used to exorcise a dybbuk without using either spells or incantations, merely with a command—with a single command! In difficult times I turn to him and he sustains me. He will not forsake me now...Call in Sender.

(MIKHOL *goes out and returns with* SENDER.)

SENDER (*arms outstretched, pleading*): Rebbe! Have pity! Save my only child!!

REB AZRIELKE: How did this terrible thing happen?

SENDER: If I remember correctly, just as the groom...

REB AZRIELKE (*interrupting him*): That's not my question. What could have cause this calamity? A worm can only penetrate into a fruit after it has alread begun to rot.

SENDER: Rebbe! My child is a God-fearing, pious daughter. She is modest and obedient.

REB AZRIELKE: Children are sometimes punished for the sins of their parents.

SENDER: If I knew of a sin I had committed, I would do penance.

REB AZRIELKE: Has anyone inquired of the dybbuk who he is and why he attached himself to your daughter?

SENDER: He won't answer. But from his voice, he was recognized as a student at our yeshiva who died quite suddenly a few months ago in the synagogue. He was meddling in the Kabbala and came to grief.

REB AZRIELKE: Through which powers?

SENDER: People say through evil ones. Just a few hours before he died, he told a friend that there was no need to wage war against sin, that there

118

was a spark of holiness in evil. He also wanted to use magic to obtain two barrels of gold.

REB AZRIELKE: Did you know him?

SENDER: Yes...As a student he used to stay at my house.

REB AZRIELKE (*looking very attentively at* SENDER): Perhaps you offended or embarrassed him? Try to remember.

SENDER: I don't know. I don't remember. (*In despair.*) Rebbe, I am only human, after all. (*Pause.*)

REB AZRIELKE: Bring the maiden.

(SENDER *goes out and returns with* FRADEH, *followed by* LAIA. LAIA *stops at the threshhold and refuses to enter.*)

SENDER (*weeping*): My child, have pity. Don't put me to shame before the rebbe. Come in.

FRADEH: Go in, Laia. Go in, my dove.

LAIA: I want to, but I cannot!

REB   Maiden, I command you to enter.

(LAIA *crosses the threshold and walks over to the table.*)

REB AZRIELKE (*continuing*): Sit down.

LAIA (*sits down obediently. Suddenly she jumps up and, with a voice not her own*): No, I won't! Leave me alone! (*She tries to run out but is stopped by* SENDER *and* FRADEH.)

REB AZRIELKE: Dybbuk, I command you to tell us who you are!

LAIA (*Dybbuk*): Rebbe of Miropolye! You know who I am. As for the others, I don't want them to know my name.

REB AZRIELKE: I am not asking for your name. I ask, who are you?

LAIA (*Dybbuk, quietly*): I am one of those who sought new paths.

REB AZRIELKE: Only he who has wandered from the straight path seeks out others.

LAIA (*Dybbuk*): That path is too narrow.

REB AZRIELKE: That was spoken by one who hasn't returned. (*Pause.*) Why did you enter the body of this maiden?

LAIA (*Dybbuk*): I am her destined bridegroom.

REB AZRIELKE: According to our holy Torah, the

122

dead are forbidden to abide among the living.

LAIA (*Dybbuk*): I am not dead.

REB AZRIELKE: You have departed from our world and you may not return until the blast of the great trumpet is sounded. Therefore, I command you to leave the body of this maiden so that a living branch of the eternal tree of Israel may not be destroyed.

LAIA (*Dybbuk, shouting*): Rebbe of Miropolye! I know how powerful and mighty you are! I know that you even have power over angels and seraphim, but you cannot control me. I have no place to go. All roads are blocked for me, and all gates shut. Evil spirits surround me from all sides, waiting to devour me. (*With a trembling voice.*) There is heaven and there is earth, and there are numberless worlds in the universe, but in not one of them can I find a resting place. And now that my embittered and harried soul has found a haven, you are trying to drive me out. Have pity! Stop pursuing me— do not drive me away.

REB AZRIEKLE: Homeless soul! Your plight overwhelms me with deepest pity, and I will do my

utmost to redeem you from your demons. But you must yield up the body of this maiden.

LAIA (*Dybbuk, firmly*): I will not!

REB AZRIELKE: Mikhol, summon a *minyen* from the synagogue.

(MIKHOL *goes out and returns immediately with* TEN MEN. *They stand at one side of the room.*)

REB AZRIELKE (*continuing*): Holy Assembly! Do you grant me the authority and power vested in you to drive a spirit out of the body of this Jewish maiden which refuses to leave her of its own accord?

ALL TEN MEN: Rebbe! We grant you our authority and the power invested in us to drive a spirit out of the body of this Jewish maiden which refuses to leave her of its own accord.

REB AZRIELKE (*rising*): Dybbuk! Soul of a being who has left our world! In the name of this Holy Assembly, and with its power, I, Azrielke, son of Hadas, command you to leave the body of the maiden, Laia bas Khanne, and in leaving to harm neither her nor any other living being. If you do not obey my command, I will proceed

against you with anathemas and excommunication, with the powers of condemnation and exorcism, with the whole might of my outstretched arm. If, however, you obey my command, I will exert every effort to reclaim your soul and drive off the evil spirits and demons which surround you.

LAIA (*Dybbuk, shrieking*): I am not afraid of your anathemas and excommunications, and I do not believe in your promises! There is no power in the world that can help me! No loftier height can compare to my present refuge, and no darker abyss to that which awaits me. I will not depart!

REB AZRIELKE: In the name of Almight God, I command you for the last time to depart. If you do not—I will be forced to excommunicate you and deliver you into the hands of the demons!

(*A frightening pause.*)

LAIA (*Dybbuk*): In the name of Almighty God, I am bound to my predestined bride and shall remain with her to eternity.

REB AZRIELKE: Mikhol, bring white shrouds for everyone in this room. Bring also seven trum-

pets and seven black candles. When you've done that, take seven Sacred Scrolls out of the Holy Ark.

(*An ominous pause during which* MIKHOL *leaves and returns with seven* shofrim* *and seven black candles. The* MESSENGER *follows him in, carrying the shrouds.*)

MESSENGER (*counting the shrouds*): There is one extra shroud. (*Looks about him.*) Is anyone missing?

REB AZRIELKE (*uneasy, as though suddenly remembering*): Before I can excommunicate a human soul, permission must be obtained from the Chief Rabbi of the city. Mikhol, for the time being, put away the trumpets, the candles and the shrouds....Mikhol, present my staff to Rabbi Shimshon and ask him, in my name, to come here directly.

(MIKHOL *gathers up the* shofrim *and candles and, together with the* MESSENGER *who is still carrying the shrouds, leaves the room.*)

---

*SHOFER; PLURAL, SHOFRIM: A RAM'S HORN BLOWN AS A TRUMPET IN BATTLE IN ANCIENT DAYS, AND USED IN SYNAGOGUES DURING ROSH HASHANA AND YOM KIPPUR.

REB AZRIELKE (*continuing; to the* TEN MEN): You may go, for the time being. (*They leave. Pause.* REB AZRIELKE *raises his head.*) Sender! Where are the bridegroom and his people?

SENDER: They stayed over at my house in Brinnits for the Sabbath.

REB AZRIELKE: Let a messenger ride to Brinnits and tell them, in my name, to wait there until they receive further word from me.

SENDER: I'll send a messenger immediately.

REB AZRIELKE: In the meantime, you may go and take your daughter into the other room.

LAIA (*awakens; in her own voice, trembling*): Grand-ma! I am afraid. What are they going to do to him? What are they going to do to me?

FRADEH: Don't be frightened, child. The rebbe knows what he's doing. He won't hurt anyone. The rebbe can't hurt anyone. (*She and Sender guide Laia into the next room.*)

REB AZRIELKE (*sits, deep in thought; suddenly, as though awakened*): And even if it has been or-dained otherwise in the upper regions, I will reverse that fateful decision.

(REB SHIMSHON *enters.*)

REB SHIMSHON: Good evening to you, Rebbe.

REB AZRIELKE (*rises and goes to greet him*): Good evening to you, too, Rabbi. Sit down. (REB SHIMSHON *seats himself.*) I have troubled you to come here because I am faced with a very serious matter. A dybbuk, God have mercy upon us, has entered the body of a Jewish maiden and under no circumstances will he release her. Our alternative is to drive him away by excommunication. I ask your permisison for this undertaking, and the merit of saving a soul will be yours.

REB SHIMSHON (*sighing*): Excommunication is a harsh enough punishment for the living; how much more so for the dead. But if there's no other way, and so godly a man as yourself finds it necessary, I grant my permission. But before your proceed, there is a secret I must reveal to you, Rebbe, which has a bearing on this affair.

REB AZRIELKE: By all means.

REB SHIMSHON: You may remember, Rebbe, it must be about twenty years ago now, a young Hassid

and Kabbalist, Nissen ben Rivke, used to come to you from Brinnits from time to time.

REB AZRIELKE: He left for some distant place and died there while still a young man.

REB SHIMSHON: Yes. Well, this very same Nissen ben Rivke appeared to me in my dreams three times last night and demanded that I summon Sender of Brinnits to trial in a Rabbinical Court.

REB AZRIELKE: What complaints has he against Sender?

REB SHIMSHON: He didn't say. He just kept claiming that Sender had spilled his blood.

REB AZRIELKE: When one Jew summons another to a Rabbinical Court, a rabbi is forbidden to refuse; especially when the complainant is dead and has resource to the Heavenly Court...But how does this have a bearing on the matter of the dybbuk?

REB SHIMSHON: It is relevant...I has come to my ears that the young man who died and who possesses Sender's daughter as a dybbuk was Nissen ben Rivke's son. There is also talk of a pact of some sort that Sender made with Nissen and didn't fulfill.

REB AZRIELKE (*reflecting for a moment*): In that case,

I shall postpone the exorcism of the dybbuk until tomorrow at noon. In the morning God willing, after prayers, we will redeem* your dreams in prayer and then you may summon the deceased to trial. Then, with your permission, I will proceed with the exorcism.

REB SHIMSHON: Since a court trial between the living and the dead is very difficult and most unusual, I should like to ask you, Rebbe, to be the chief judge and to conduct the trial.

REB AZRIELKE: Very well. Mikhol! (MIKHOL *enters.*) Have the maiden brought in.

(SENDER *and* FRADEH *bring* LAIA *in. She sits with her eyes shut.*)

REB AZRIELKE (*continuing*): Dybbuk, you have another twenty-four hours. If, by the appointed hour, you haven't left of your own free will, I shall by permission granted me by the Chief Rabbi, expel you by an act of excommunication. (*Pause.* SENDER *and* FRADEH *begin to lead* LAIA *out.*) Sender, stay here. (FRADEH *leads* LAIA

*SPECIAL PRAYERS THAT ARE REPEATED AFTER A PERSON HAS DREAMT, IN ORDER TO REMOVE ANY BAD OMEN THE DREAM MAY CONTAIN. THE FOURTH ACT BEGINS WITH THE RECITATION OF THIS PRAYER.

out.) Sender, do you remember your old friend, Nissen ben Rivke?

SENDER (*frightened*): Nissen ben Rivke? He died...

REB AZRIELKE: Know, then, that he appeared three times last night in a dream to the Chief Rabbi. (*Points to* REB SHIMSHON.) He demanded that you be summoned to a Rabbinical Court trial with him.

SENDER (*entirely shaken*): Me? To a trial? Woe is me! What does he want of me? What shall I do, Rebbe?

REB AZRIELKE: I don't know what he is accusing you of, but you must accept the summons.

SENDER: I will do as you say.

REB AZRIELKE (*in a different tone of voice*): Send a team of the swiftest horses directly and speedily to Brinnits to bring the bridegroom and his people. I want them here by tomorrow noon so that the wedding may take place as soon as the dybbuk is exorcised.

SENDER: Rebbe. What if they don't want to go through with the marriage and refuse to come?

(*The* MESSENGER *appears at the door.*)

REB AZRIELKE (*authoritatively*): Tell them I have commanded it. See to it that the bridegroom is here on time.

MESSENGER: The bridegroom will be here on time.

(*The clock strikes twelve.*)

(*Curtain.*)

Act Four

Same room as in Act Three. Instead of the long table on the left, a smaller one is closer to the footlights. An armchair and two ordinary chairs behind the table are occupied by REB AZRIELKE, wearing a prayer shawl and phylacteries, and the TWO JUDGES. RABBI SHIMSHON stands at the side of the table; and in the back stands MIKHOL. They are reciting the prayer to ensure that dreams come to a good conclusion.

REB SHIMSHON: May the dream be a good omen! May the dream be a good omen!

REB AZRIELKE, TWO JUDGES (*together*): May your dream be a good omen! May your dream be a good omen!

133

REB AZRIELKE: Now that we have blessed your dream, Rabbi, sit here with the other judges. (REB SHIMSHON *takes a seat at the table, next to* REB AZRIELKE.) Let us summon the deceased. But first I must draw a circle beyond which he may not venture. Mikhol, bring me my cane. (MIKHOL *gives him the cane.* REB AZRIELKE *rises, walks over to the left corner of the room and describes a circle, from left to right. Then he goes back to his place at the table.*) Mikhol, take my cane and go to the cemetery. Once you get there, close your eyes and, holding the cane before you, start walking. Stop at the first grave the cane touches. Knock on the grave three times and repeat these works: "Blameless departed! Azrielke, son of the saintly Reb Itchele of Miropolye, sent me to ask your forgiveness for disturbing your rest. He commands you to inform the blameless deceased, Nissen ben Rivke, by ways that are known to you, that the just Rabbinical Court of Miropolye summons him immediately to a court trial and desires him to wear the garments in which he was buried." Say these words three times; then return here. Do not look back whatever cries or shrieks or calls you may hear. And do not let my cane fall from your hands, even for an in-

stant, or you are in great peril. Go and God will protect you; for no harm can come to messengers on a virtuous errand. But, before you go, have two men make a partition to separate the dead from the living.

(MIKHOL *leaves. Two men enter, carrying a sheet. They partition off the entire left corner of the room all the way to the floor and leave.*)

REB AZRIELKE: Call in Sender (SENDER *comes in.*) Sender, have you accomplished what I instructed you to do? Did you send a team of horses to fetch the bridegroom and his people?

SENDER: I sent men on swiftest horses, but they have not yet returned.

REB AZRIELKE: Send a messenger on horseback to tell them to hurry.

SENDER: I will (*Pause.*)

REB AZRIELKE: Sender, we have sent word to the blameless deceased, Nissen ben Rivke, that the Rabbinical Court summons him to trial with you. Will you accept our verdict?

SENDER: I will accept it.

135

REB AZRIELKE: Will you carry out our decision?

SENDER: I will carry it out.

REB AZRIELKE: Go, then, and take your place at the right.

SENDER: Rebbe! I remember now...Nissen ben Rivke must be summoning me to stand trial on account of a pact we made. But I am not at fault in the matter.

REB AZRIELKE: You will tell us about that later, after the deceased has informed us of his complaint. (*Pause.*) A man will soon appear before us who comes from the True World, in order to stand trial with a man from our world of illusion. (*Pause.*) A trial such as this demonstrates the power of our Holy Torah over all worlds and all created things, and is binding upon both the living and the dead. (*Pause.*) A trial such as this is most difficult and fearsome. All the spheres of creation have their eyes turned upon it. And should this court, God forbid, deviate from the law by even a hair's breadth, a clamour will arise in the Heavenly Court above. One must approach such a trial with fear and trembling...fear...and trepidation. (*Looks about him uneasily, his gaze stops at the partition and*

he falls silent. A frightening quiet ensues.)

FIRST JUDGE (*to the* SECOND JUDGE *in a low and frightened voice*): I think he has come.

SECOND JUDGE (*in the same tone of voice*): I think he has.

REB SHIMSHON: He is here.

REB AZRIELKE: Blameless deceased Nissen ben Rivke, this just Rabbinical Court has decreed that you enter the circle and partition set up for you and that you not go beyond. (*Pause.*) Blameless deceased Nissen ben Rivke, this just Rabbinical Court commands you to state your complaint and grievance against Sender ben Henye.

(*A frightening pause. All sit as though turned to stone.*)

FIRST JUDGE (*as before*): I think he is answering.

SECOND JUDGE: It seems so.

FIRST JUDGE: I hear a voice, but no words.

SECOND JUDGE: I hear words, but no voice.

REB SHIMSHON (*To* SENDER): Sender ben Henye! The blameless deceased Nissen ben Rivke claims and

states that in your youth you and he were students at the same yeshiva, and your souls were bound to each other in the ties of true friendship. Both of you were married in the same week. Later when you met at the rebbe's house during the High Holy Days, you made a pact with each other, pledging that, should your wives conceive and one give birth to a son and the other to a daughter, the children would be wed.

SENDER (*in a quavering voice*): Yes, that is how it was.

REB SHIMSHON: The blameless deceased Nissen ben Rivke states further that, subsequently, he left for some distant town where his wife gave birth to a son at the same time that your wife gave birth to a daughter. He died soon after. (*Short pause.*) In the True World he learned that his son had been blessed with a lofty soul and was ascending upwards, stage by stage. Hearing this, he was filled with paternal pride and joy. He also observed that when his son became older, he began to wander all over the world, from place to place, from country to country, from city to city, for his soul yearned for his predestined bride. And he arrived at the city

where you live, he came to your house and sat at your table. And his soul was bound to the soul of your daughter. But you were rich, and Nissen's son was poor. And you turned away from him and sought out a bridegroom for your daughter from among the wealthy and proud families. (*Short pause.*) Nissen then observed that his son was becoming despondent and that he wandered about the world, seeking new paths, and his paternal soul was permeated with uneasiness and sorrow. And the Power of Darkness perceived the youth's utter desperation and, spreading its net before him, entrapped him and snatched him from the world before his time; and his soul roamed about, lost, until it passed into the body of his predestined bride as a dybbuk. (*Short pause.*) Nissen ben Rivke declares: with the death of his son, he has been severed from both worlds; he is without a name and without a memorial; without an heir and without a mourner to recite the Kaddish prayer for his soul. His light has been dimmed forever and his crown rolled down into the abyss. He pleads that this just Rabbinical Court judge Sender according to the laws of our Holy Torah, for spilling the blood of Nissen's son and of his son's sons unto the end of all generations.

(*Frightening silence.* SENDER *sobs.*)

REB AZRIELKE: Sender ben Henye. Did you hear the charges of the blameless deceased, Nissen ben Rivke? What is your reply?

SENDER: I cannot speak...There are no words to defend myself. I beg my old friend to forgive me for this sin—my intentions were not evil. Nissen left soon after our pact was made, and I had no way of knowing whether his wife gave birth to a child at all, and if she did, whether it was a son or a daughter. I discovered later that he had died. I had no other word about him or his family, and the whole matter gradually slipped from my mind.

REB AZRIELKE: Why didn't you inquire? Why didn't you investigate further?

SENDER: Usually the bridegroom's family takes the first step. I believed that if Nissen had had a son, he would have informed me. (*Pause.*)

REB SHIMSHON: Nissen ben Rivke would like to know why, when his son entered your house and sat at your table, you never asked him who he was and anything about his family.

140

SENDER: I don't know...I don't remember...But I swear something always kept telling me to choose him as my son-in-law. That's why I made such difficult conditions every time a match was proposed that the groom's family usually refused to comply. Three matches fell through in this way. This time the family agreed to the conditions...(*Pause.*)

REB SHIMSHON: Nissen ben Rivke says that deep in your innermost being you recognized his son and were afraid to ask him who he was, because you sought a life of ease and wealth for your daughter, and that's why you pushed his son into the abyss.

(SENDER, *his face covered with his hands, weeps silently. Long pause.* MIKHOL *enters and returns the staff to* REB AZRIELKE.)

REB AZRIELKE (*speaks softly with* REB SHIMSHON *and the* JUDGES, *then rises and takes the staff in his hand*): This just Rabbinical Court has heard both sides of the case and delivers the following verdict:

Whereas it is not known whether, at the time the agreement between Nissen ben Rivke and

Sender ben Henye was made, their wives had already conceived; and whereas, according to our Holy Torah, no agreement can be considered valid that involves something not yet in existence, we cannot, therefore, conclude that Sender was compelled to fulfill the agreement. But since the Upper Spheres accepted the agreement as valid and implanted the belief in the heart of Nissen ben Rivke's son that Sender ben Henye's daughter was his predestined bride; and since Sender's subsequent actions resulted in misfortune for Nissen ben Rivke and his son— this just Rabbinical Court decrees that Sender must donate half his fortune to the poor and, for the rest of his life, light the memorial candle and recite the Kaddish prayer for Nissen ben Rivke and his son, as though they were his own kin. (*Pause.*) This just Rabbinical Court asks the blameless deceased, Nissen ben Rivke, to forgive Sender unconditionally; and, further, requests that, as a father, he command his son to leave the body of the maiden, Laia bas Khanne, so that a branch of the fruitful tree of Israel may not wither. In consequence of this, the Almighty will make manifest His great mercy to Nissen ben Rivke and to his homeless son.

ALL: Amen! (*Pause.*)

REB AZRIELKE: Blameless deceased, Nissen ben Rivke. Did you hear our verdict? Do you accept it? (*A suspenseful pause.*) Sender ben Henye. Did you hear our verdict? Do you accept it?

SENDER: Yes, I accept it.

REB AZRIELKE: Blameless deceased, Nissen ben Rivke. The trial between you and Sender ben Henye is now over. You must now return to your place of rest. We decree that, in going, you shall injure neither man nor any other living creature. (*Pause.*) Mikhol! Have the partition removed and bring some water.

(MIKHOL *calls in two people who remove the partition.* REB AZRIELKE *makes a circle with his staff at the same spot as before, but from right to left. A basin and dipper are brought in and all wash their hands.*)

REB AZRIELKE (*continuing*): Sender, have the bridegroom and his family arrived?

SENDER: Not a sign of their arrival as yet.

REB AZRIELKE: Send another messenger to tell them to ride with all possible speed. Have the canopy

put up and the musicians ready. Have the bride dressed in her wedding gown so that as soon as the dybbuk is exorcised, she may be led under the canopy. That which was to have been—may it be done!

(SENDER *leaves.* REB AZRIELKE *takes off his prayer shawl and phylacteries and puts them away.*)

REB SHIMSHON (*in whispers to the* JUDGES): Did you notice that the deceased did not forgive Sender?

FIRST AND SECOND JUDGES (*softly, frightened*): We did.

REB SHIMSHON: Did you realize that the deceased did not accept the verdict?

FIRST AND SECOND JUDGES: We did.

REB SHIMSHON: Did you sense that he did not say Amen to Reb Azrielke's words?

FIRST AND SECOND JUDGES: We sensed it.

REB SHIMSHON: That's a very bad omen.

FIRST AND SECOND JUDGES: Yes, it is.

REB SHIMSHON: See how disturbed Reb Azrielke is.

His hands are trembling. (*Pause.*) We have done our part and we may leave now.

(*The* Judges *quietly leave, unnoticed.* Reb Shimshon *prepares to leave also.*)

Reb Azrielke: Rabbi. Stay until the dybbuk is driven out. I should like you to perform the wedding ceremony. (Reb Shimshon *sighs and, with downcast head, sits down to a side. An oppressive pause.*) Lord of the Universe! Hidden and marvelous are Thy ways. But the path I walk is illuminated by the light from the flame of Thy divine will and I shall not stray from it, neither to the right nor to the left. (*Lifting his head.*) Mikhol, is everything ready?

Mikhol: Yes, Rebbe.

Reb Azrielke: Have the maiden brought in. (Sender *and* Fradeh *lead* Laia *in; she is dressed in a white wedding gown and a black cloak is thrown over her shoulders. They seat her on the sofa...*Rabbi Shimshon *takes a seat beside* Reb Azrielke.) Dybbuk! In the name of the Chief Rabbi of this city, seated here, in the name of the holy Assembly of Men, in the name of the great Sanhedrin of Jerusalem, I, Azrielke ben

Hadas, order you for the last time to leave the body of the maiden, Laia bas Khanne!

LAIA (*Dybbuk, decisively*): I shall not leave!

REB AZRIELKE: Mikhol, call the people in and bring the shrouds, the trumpets and the black candles. (MIKHOL *goes out and returns with fifteen men, among them the* MESSENGER. *They carry in shrouds, shofrim and candles.*) Bring out the Scrolls. (MIKHOL *removes seven Holy Scrolls, distributes them among seven men and then distributes the seven shofrim to the remaining worshipers.*) Obdurate spirit! Since you refuse to obey our command, I deliver you into the hands of the higher spirits who will expel you by force. Sound a blast! *Tekia!*

(*They sound the notes "tekia."*)

LAIA (*leaps from her seat, shaking violently and in the Dybbuk's voice, shouting*): Leave me alone! Stop pulling at me! I won't go! I can't go!

REB AZRIELKE: Since the spirits of the Higher Sphere are not able to vanquish you, I entrust you into the hands of the spirits of the Middle Sphere— those that are neither good nor evil—let them drive you out. Sound *sh'vorim!*

(*The shofrim sound the notes "sh'vorim."*)

LAIA (*Dybbuk, with waning strength*): Woe is me! All the powers of the world are gathered against me. Terrible demons without mercy are pulling at me. Arrayed against me and commanding me to depart are the souls of the great and the just, and my father's soul among them. But, as long as a single spark of strength remains within me, I will struggle, and I will not depart.

REB AZRIELKE (*to himself*): It can only be that some mighty power is helping him! (*Pause.*) Mikhol. Put the Scrolls back into the Holy Ark. (*They are put back.*) Cover the Holy Ark with a black curtain. (MIKHOL *does so.*) Light the black candles. (*That is done.*) Let everyone put on the white shrouds. (*Everyone, including* REB AZRIELKE *and* RABBI SHIMSHON, *do so.* REB AZRIELKE *lifts his hand high and in a loud and terrifying voice proclaims*) Rise up, O Lord! Let thine enemies be scattered and dispersed. Thou sinful and stubborn spirit! With the power of Almighty God and with the supreme authority of the Holy Torah, I, Azrielke ben Hadas, tear asunder every thread that binds you to the

living world and to the body and soul of the maiden, Laia bas Khanne!

LAIA (*Dybbuk, cries out*): Woe is me!

REB ARZIELKE: And I excommunicate you from the people of Israel! Trumpets! *Teruah.*

MESSENGER: The last spark has fused with the flame.

LAIA (*Dybbuk, without strength*): I can struggle no longer.

(*The shofrim sound the notes "teruah."*)

REB AZRIELKE (*silencing the shofrim with a show of his hand; to Laia*): Do you submit?

LAIA (*Dybbuk, in a lifeless voice*): I submit.

REB AZRIELKE: Do you promise of your own free will to leave the body of the maiden, Laia bas Khanne, never to return?

LAIA (*Dybbuk, as before*): I promise.

REB AZRIELKE: By the same power and authority granted me to place you under the ban of excommunication, I now lift that ban. (*To* MIKHOL.) Put away the trumpets. (MIKHOL *gathers them up and puts them away.*) The

150

others may now remove their shrouds and leave. (*The fourteen men take off the shrouds and leave with the* MESSENGER *and* MIKHOL. REB AZRIELKE *raises his arms high.*) Lord of the Universe! God of mercy and grace! Behold the great suffering of this homeless and tortured soul; a soul which fell because of the sins and errors of others. Consider not its misdeeds but let its former virtues, its present torments, and the merits of its forebears rise before Thee like an obscuring vapor. Lord of the Universe, clear its path of evil spirits and prepare for it eternal rest in Thy palaces. Amen.

ALL: Amen!

LAIA (*shaking violently, in the Dybbuk's voice*): Recite the Kaddish for me. My appointed time is running out.

REB AZRIELKE: Sender! Recite the first Kaddish.

SENDER: *Yisgadal, veyiskadash shemei rabba. B'almah div'rah khireisei...*

(*The clock strikes twelve.*)

LAIA (*springs up, in Dybbuk's voice*): Ei-eiy! (*Falls back to the sofa as if in a faint.*)

REB AZRIELKE: Lead the bride to the canopy.

(MIKHOL *runs in.*)

MIKHOL (*extremely upset*): The second rider has just
    returned. He says that a wheel broke on the
    bridegroom's carriage so they are coming the
    rest of the way on foot. But they're pretty close
    now, on the hill. You can see them from here.

REB AZRIELKE (*extremely disturbed*): What was to
    have been, shall be! (*To* SENDER.) Let the old
    woman remain here with the bride and let us
    go out to welcome the bridegroom.

(*With his staff, he draws a circle round* LAIA *from
left to right. He takes off the shroud and hangs it
near the door. He leaves the room with his staff in
hand.* SENDER *and* MIKHOL *follow him out. A long
pause.*)

LAIA (*wakes; in a very weak voice*): Who is here
    with me? Is that you, Granny? Granny? My
    heart is so heavy. Help me. Cuddle me.

FRADEH (*caressing her*): Don't be sad, my child. Let
    the Cossacks be sad or the black cat, but let
    your heart be as light as a feather, like a puff of

breath, like a snowflake, and may little angels
cradle you in their little wings.

*(The orchestra is heard from the distance, playing
the wedding march.)*

LAIA *(frightened; she grasps* FRADEH's *hand)*: Do you
 hear that? They are going to dance around the
 holy grave of the dead bride and groom, to
 cheer them up.

FRADEH: Don't tremble, child. Don't be afraid. A
 great and mighty force is standing guard over
 you. Sixty giants with drawn swords are watching over you. Our holy patriarchs are shielding
 you from the evil eye. *(Gradually she drifts into
 a ballad-like song.)*

Soon they shall lead you under the canopy,
Happy and blessed that hour will be.
Your saintly mother comes here from Paradise,
Bedecked in robes of silver and gold.
Greeting your mother are two angels bright,
Two angels bright,
They will take her by the hands,
One the left, and one the right.
 "Khannele mine, Khannele mine!

153

Why have you come decked in robes so fine?"
And this is what Khannele answers and says:
"No robes are too fine for this day of days!
My only child, the crown of my head,
This day will to the canopy be led."
    "Khannele mine, Khannele mine!
Why is your face in pain and sorrow entwined?"
And this is what Khannele answers and says:
"What sorrow too great for this day of days!
My daughter is led by others to her wedding in
    in pride
And I must in sorrow stand aside..."
When to the canopy they lead the bride,
Young and old will come from every side,
And the Prophet Elijah takes his goblet of wine,
Reciting the blessing, himself, for the wine.
And then—
The whole land will echo: Amen. Amen.

(FRADEH *falls asleep. Long pause.*)

LAIA (*her eyes closed. Sighs deeply, and opens her eyes*): Who sighed with such pain?

VOICE OF KHONNON: I.

LAIA: I hear your voice, but I don't see you.

VOICE OF KHONNON: You are fenced off from me by an enchanted circle.

LAIA: Your voice sounds as sweet as the cry of a violin on a silent night. Tell me. Who are you?

VOICE OF KHONNON: I have forgotten...It is only through your thoughts that I can remember who I am...

LAIA: I remember now. My heart yearned toward a radiant star....On silent nights I shed many sweet tears, and there was a figure always in my dreams. Was that you?

VOICE OF KHONNON: Yes.

LAIA: I remember...Your hair was soft and gleaming as though touched with tears, your eyes gentle and melancholy...Your hands with long, slender fingers. Awake or asleep—I thought only of you. (*Pause. Sadly.*) But you went away, and I lived in darkness. My soul was forlorn and I was like a desolate widow pursued by strangers. And then you returned, and my heart blossomed anew and sorrow turned to joy. Why did you forsake me again?

VOICE OF KHONNON: I destroyed all barriers and rose above death. I defied the laws of the ages and

generations. I struggled with the powerful, the mighty, and the merciless. And when the last spark of my strength was spent, I left your body to return to your soul.

LAIA (*tenderly*): Come back to me, my bridegroom, my husband. I will bear you, in death, in my heart; and in our dreams at night, we will both rock our unborn little babes to sleep. (*Weeps.*) We will sew little shirts for them to wear and sing them lullabies. (*Sings, weeping.*)

> *Hush, hush, little ones,*
> *Without cradle, without clothes,*
> *Dead you are and still unborn,*
> *Timeless and forever lost...*

(*A wedding march is heard approaching from the distance.*)

LAIA (*trembling*): They are coming to take me to the canopy with a stranger! Come to me, my bridegroom!

VOICE OF KHONNON: I have left your body and will come to your soul.

(*He is seen in white against the wall.*)

LAIA (*with joy*): The barriers of the circle are broken! I see you, my bridegroom! Come to me!

KHONNON (*like an echo*): Come to me!

LAIA (*crying out with joy*): I am coming...

KHONNON (*like an echo*): I am coming...

VOICES (*from outside*): Lead the bride to the canopy!

(*A wedding march. LAIA, dropping her black cloak on the sofa and now arrayed completely in white, walks in step to the wedding music to KHONNON. She stops at the spot where he appeared and their two figures merge. REB AZRIELKE enters, staff in hand, followed by the MESSENGER. They stop at the door. Behind them, SENDER, FRADEH and the others.*)

LAIA (*in a voice that appears to come from the far distance*): A great light is flowing all about me. I am bound to you forever, my predestined... Together we will soar higher, and higher, and higher...

(*The stage grows gradually darker.*)

REB AZRIELKE (*lowering his head*): Too late...

MESSENGER: Blessed be the True Judge.

*(The stage is thrown into complete darkness. From
the distance is heard very softly:)*

> *Wherefore, O wherefore*
> *Has the soul*
> *Fallen from exalted heights*
> *To profoundest depths?*
> *Within itself, the fall*
> *Contains the ascension.*

(Curtain)

This book was set by The Works in twelve point Palatino
on a Compugraphic Compuwriter II and edited by Ruth Glushanok.
Book design and calligraphy are by
Kadi Karist Tint.